A Wyrm In The Heart

By Matt Kirkby

Table of Contents

Chapter One

The arrow flights falter as the Norse archers stand open-mouthed as the foul-smelling smoke begins to clear. Ragged craters mar the grass. Moans and shrieks rise from the wounded, loud in the sudden stillness. The Harfleurs' own retainer also stare and several of my chosen throwers take hasty steps away from the unused jugs stored at their feet.

"I guard this place!" I shout to the heavens. "I ward this land and my shield is strong." I hastily climb atop a barrel and gesture threateningly at the motionless foe, the top of the palisade now reaching only to my knees. "Thou call thyselves a scourge?" Every eye is upon me, even my own retainers. "I spit upon thy graves and mock thy gods." The wind picks up, making my cloak flap violently. "Fear my wrath, Norsemen, and flee whilst thou may!" I gesture to my throwers. "Strike them again!"

A second group of pottery jugs falls into their midst and more explosions ring out.

I laugh as the startled Norsemen abandon their charge and hastily turn to flee back beyond thrown-jug range and then beyond arrow range.

"A little Dragon's Bane is a handy thing indeed." My voice betrays my amusement at the sight.

A proud mob turned into a disorganized rabble and sent scurrying away with their tails between their legs. "A handful of old women could have routed them."

"'Twas dark sorcery!" Bastian curses as wisps of sulphurous smoke drift past us on the wind.

He has only just arrived, climbing into the tower while I was declaiming with such theatrics.

I shake my head. "Nay, 'twas but a little alchemy I read about. Much like herb craft save I use mineral salts rather than plant leaves and flowers."

"'Twas still effective whatever its source." Bastian shakes his head in amazement. "Mayhap our Lord Himself do fight on our behalf."

I roll my eyes. "I will believe that event when I see it with my own eyes." I stare down at the torn ground which stretches away from the ditch towards the forest. Smoke rises from a score of craters blasted into the dirt. Men lay there, broken. Many of them are moaning or crying out piteously.

The stench of sulphur and blood and fear is enough to choke me. "This be a most foul weapon though.

Dragon's Bane. 'Tis more like something thy Christian Devil would wield."

Bastian eyes me.

I take care not to smile too widely back at him.

* * *

"What is keeping that accursed Count!"

Lurking in the shadows beside a wagon, I smile to myself. It seems that Ulric has indeed taken note of the failure of his supposed ally to supply the Witch King with the sudden surrender of both the village and its Keep.

"We had a deal. He knew well enough that he was to strike the heir ere the moon rose yesterday. The Keep should be wailing with misery and sorrow."

I slip closer to the tent. Norsemen are bustling and moving about their camp, but none have yet taken any overt notice of me. The proper attitude is all the disguise that I need, that and a proper cloak and helmet that I still have from my previous foray into the tents. Stealing them from the war leader had been a wise idea for me.

It had been simple child's play for me to slip out of the village via a rope slung over the palisade. Charles had seen the necessity of my sortie, and eventually convinced Bastian to accede to the wisdom of my going alone. No other man present could match me in stealth.

Well, I suspect that Livia could but she had refused to accompany me. "'Tis not ladylike," she had protested. "I will remain and watch over thy friend, Charles." With the aid of a long rope, I had climbed down the almost sheer cliff to the narrow western beach—ledge really—and thus skirt along the edge of the otherwise deserted shoreline to come upon the Norse camp from the northwest. Their sentries had been far more concerned with watching for a splashy sortie from the village than from a single man slipping into their midst from the flanks.

And now here I stand not ten paces from their leader.

All too easy.

"I will not be forgiving of such failure when we take the Keep. This foolish nobleman," he makes the name a curse, "will rue the day that he dared dream of challenging me."

"Aye, my Lord."

I do not recognize that deep voice, coming from inside the grey cloth tent, but I can picture his type well enough in my mind. Brawny and hulking, with more muscles than brains methinks.

"Sven, I will rely closely upon thy services in the final assault." Ulric's voice has grown calm, almost seductive in tone. "It will be up to thy warriors to distract the men of the garrison after my magick has breached the Keep's defenses and toppled its wall."

I creep closer to the tent. The weave of the fabric is coarse, no doubt waterproofed in some fashion. The colour is a faded grey, like the hues of a deep fog. A cold gust of wind tugs at my cloak.

The colour might also be that of a shroud from a corpse two moons buried methinks.

"And my berserkers will be up to the challenge, my Lord. No man shall stand in our path and live to see the dawn."

"I have no fear of that fact." Ulric sounds confident. Mayhap too confident. "And to ensure thy success, I will supply thee with a potent draught of my own design. As I cast my magicks, thy men will drink deeply of it and thus will the spell be made complete. Thy berserkers will fight with the ferocity of wild animals." He chuckles, the chilling sound of someone's death rattle.

"When do we launch the attack?" Sven sounds eager, like a trained dog waiting for the order to tear the throat from his prey with bloodstained jaws.

"Soon. The omens are not yet favorable. But they soon will be, Sven. Ere long they will be totally in my favour." Ulric's voice has taken on a dreamy, almost distracted, quality. "Leave me."

Standing as still as a statue, I watch Sven—a hulking, muscular brute of a man—throw open the flap of the tent from within and emerge into the dark night to stride past me without noticing my presence in the slightest.

I allow him a few moments to wander away into the depths of the camp, and then I step into the tent, holding up the gray fabric covering the doorway with my hand. "A moment of your time, Ulric?"

The tent is small and cramped, lit by a pair of flickering candles held in place on a small table by their own melted wax. The floor is piled with brightly-woven carpets. The air of must and decay is heavy here, as if the furnishings and the tent's lone occupant are crumbling away even as I watch.

The Witch King is kneeling on the carpets. "Yes?" he asks, without looking up from the crystal sphere held before him in his cupped hands. Light sparkles from the sphere and splashes across his face. "What do thou want of me now?"

"I bear urgent tidings for ye."

At my voice, Ulric looks up at last. "What be possibly so urgent that thou would dare to disturb my nightly meditations? Thou?" His green eyes bulge and his face pales. He knows my face and that knowledge seems to chill him to his very soul. "Faith! 'Tis thee!" he stammers, closing his gaping mouth. He staggers to his feet, blinking his eyes repeatedly as if I am some figment of his imagination that he can banish at will.

"Aye, 'tis me indeed." I smile at him, making my polite grin into a mocking sneer. "Do not bother to call for help, for thou will be dead ere any of thy minions can arrive to aid thee."

Ulric sets the crystal sphere onto the table and turns to face me fully. "I am but a humble old man," he tells me in a cracked voice. "What harm can I do to one such as thee?" He spreads his arms wide, showing me his empty hands, though his black robes might hide any number of weapons within their folds.

"Plenty, I dare think." I keep one hand on my sword hilt—to better cow him though I have little interest in using my sword on him. The table is the only piece of furniture other than a mound of blankets piled carelessly in a corner as a rough bed. 'Tis more like a nest for some burrowing animal than a bed for a man.

"Then what is thy urgent news for me? What message do thou bring to me here, in the heart of my own camp?" Ulric picks up a small goblet from the table; it looks like carefully worked silver. He raises it to his lips and sips from it. "Some water? 'Tis pure and clean and cool." His lips twitch in a smile. "I swear to thee that it be not poisoned."

I shake my head in refusal. "Richard D'Erlette presently holds court within the dungeons of Keep Harfleur, Ulric. He is of no further use to thee. We know the details to all thy foul plans."

"Do ye? Mayhap he has nothing to do with me or with my supposed plans. Mayhap he made up such a tale to entice thee? A madman perhaps? Thou would trust the word of a turncoat then?"

"Over thy lies? Yes, I would."

"I see." Ulric shakes his head. "And now thou no doubt expect me to obey thy commands and surrender my army to thee? Exile ourselves back to the Norselands?" He laughs, a mocking sound to his amusement. "I fear that thou overrate thy skills, sellsword." The contempt in his voice is every bit as sharp as Shadow's Kiss.

"I am more than a mere sellsword, Witch King." I allow a hint of the rage within my to light my eyes with a baleful inner fire. "I could slay thee and half of thy minions ere they know of my presence amongst them."

"If thou truly possessed such powers, then thou would use them!" Ulric mocks me, unfazed by my glare. "Thy pretty little tricks will not avail thee." He mimics some of the gestures I had made upon my tower perch. "Instead I will teach thou what true power can do." He gestures with his right hand at the table. "Draconis!"

With my enhanced eyesight, I can see him toss a powder into a flagon of what looks to be pure water.

And then the light of the noontime sun itself blazes forth from the water.

"Gah!" I raise my hand to shield my eyes, cursing. I can hear footsteps scurrying away—Ulric is escaping!

The glow fades and I am able to see again, barely. Squinting and pawing at my eyes, I stagger through the tent flap and see Ulric hurrying towards a cluster of his followers.

"Guards!" Ulric shouts. "Slay him!"

I hear the sound of booted feet over Ulric's shout and I can see Norsemen approaching me from many directions in answer to their master's call. For a moment I caress the hilt of Shadow's Kiss.

"Damnation!" There are too many to fight. Far too many. And Ulric himself is now beyond my reach.

With a snarl, I turn and run towards the Keep. When pressed I have heard others of my Kind claim that they can outrun a horse...now I shall see if that is indeed the case.

Chapter Two

"I know not what to council ye." Charles calmly states from where he lays in his bed, under several warm blankets, with his back propped up by several pillows. The candles lighting his bedchamber are scenting the air with honey. "I did not foresee this betrayal."

"D'Erlette has a rot, a worm in his heart." The healer women have allowed us some time to speak with Charles, believing that he will heal more quickly if he might at least hear how the siege fares, rather than endure alone in his chambers bereft of news. "It is a corruption that might have consumed thy lands." We are under strict orders not to tire him out though, under pain of censure. I am not certain what the healers might do to us should we disobey their commands, but I long ago took a blood oath not to trouble anyone who knows the arts of blending herbs. No, not after the stomach cramps and fevers which came as the aftermath of one particular practical joke from my youth.

"The Count is safely within our dungeons and his men have either sworn allegiance to us, or else fled or perished when we sought their capture." Bastian shakes his head grimly. "Most foreswore their count when word of his betrayal spread, seeking to serve us and regain their honor."

"And yet some did not." I had helped hunt down three of D'Erlette's retainers who had sought to flee the Keep. They had tried to take a child hostage and use him as a shield to barter their freedom.

They had tasted sour, their essence weak and watery. "Some have perished in attempts at scaling the cliffs."

"This place is a natural fortress, easy to defend given that any foe might only approach from one side." Charles smiles. "No man can scale the cliffs without a rope and no man in the village would aid the Norsemen in breaching our defenses." While speaking with us, his face has regained much of its color. I almost think that he recover fully if we dressed him in his armor and then followed him to the battlefield.

"I cannot foresee any such betrayal. Thou are beloved by thy people. None here will aid Ulric."

"Ulric." The name seems sour in Charles' mouth. "Thou must tell me more of this Witch King.

How might he have gained such dominance and power over the Norsemen?"

"That be a mystery." It has puzzled me for some time. "He is a sorcerer of not inconsiderable talent from what I have heard thus far. Whilst moving through his camp I heard talk of his powers."

"What powers?"

"He has summoned lighting to strike at his foes. He casts forth plague." That could also mean that he simply poisons his foes. "I overheard many tales and stories. Rumors fester amongst those tents like mould. I fear that the entire answer lies in the frozen wastes of the northlands."

There is a soft knock at the door. Bastian opens it. "Yes?"

"My lords," the young man-at-arms offers a hasty bow. "I bear word from the palisade.

Something is happening within the Norse camp."

"What?"

"We are not certain. They appear to be stirring."

"Mayhap 'tis the prelude to another attack." I stand up. "I must go, Charles."

"Aye. Would that I could accompany ye." He coughs weakly. "Would that I had the strength to ride into battle at thy side and together we might slay many of the foe."

"Shadow's Kiss shall slay foes in thy name tonight," I tell him.

Bastian smiles warmly. "Thou will recover ere long, Father."

"Heed Franc's advice," the elder Harfleur warns. "He be learned and experienced in the arts of war."

"So I have learned thus far. I will trust him as thou trust him." Bastian gestures towards the edge of the village. "Coming?"

"Aye." I nod a farewell to Charles. "Until later."

"Cum Saxum Saxorum. Induersum montum oparium da—in Aetibulum, in Quinatum, Draconis!" Ulric gestures wildly as the fire crackles to life. The flames rise up around him, wreathing him in columns of blazing fire while the chill wind whips at his midnight-black robes. "Erce, erce, erce! I invoke you, Powers of Air, Kingdom of Wind! Behold: Gorias, Esras, Paruldas!"

His voice echoes clearly to us as the wind lulls for a brief moment. And then the next gust tries to blow us from the parapet where we stand watching the wizard work.

"He be up to something."

"Of course he is, Bastian." I frown at the black-robed figure dancing amid three raging bonfires whilst a handful of Norsemen beat drums in a steady rhythm. "It's a spell." I know the words vaguely.... "He is summoning the Elemental Lords to augment his own magick." Twilight has fallen while the Norsemen stacked firewood into large pyres and prepared it for burning. And now they stand in a number of tight groups, watching their master perform his sinister ritual.

"That would not be a good thing."

"Nay, my friend." My fingers tighten their grip on the stone wall as black storm clouds blow in from the north to slowly cover the star-strewn sky with their shroud. "'Tis not a good thing at all." A storm is brewing...how ill-timed.

"I am still amazed that thou were able to escape from his camp yesterday eve."

"I am swift of foot." I think that I did manage to run faster than a horse, faster than I have seen Tempest gallop. "And I was devious." I had used my Norse disguise to buy myself a few precious moments of confusion in the camp ere my identity became widely known. "Plus I knew that thy archers would give me aid in my approach. Once I was within bowshot of the walls, I was quite safe."

Bastian smiles. "Only a few of thy pursuers came close to thee."

"Aye." A few too many, I think, for one thrusting spear had nearly spitted me like a boar being prepared for roasting ere I had outpaced them. "Thy archers are well skilled." They had slain at least four Norsemen and not a single shaft had even flown close to me.

"Anail Nathrock. Uthas Bethudd. Dochiel Dienve." The words come to us again between gusts of wind. "Anail Nathrock. Uthas Bethudd. Dochiel Dienve!" Ulric shouts over the howling of the wind.

The sky overhead has darkened even further and now rain begins to fall. Lightning flashes brightly, rending through the clouds, and thunder booms out loud enough the shake the stone walls of the Keep itself.

"What manner of storm be this?" Bastian demands as he pulls his cloak more tightly around his body. "To have come upon us so quickly, it cannot be natural!" The rain is pounding down.

"'Tis a fierce one." I try to calm my nerves. The air feels...wrong somehow.

"'Tis a most unnatural storm," one of the men-at-arms mutters. He wipes rain from his face.

"He cannot mean to fight tonight," Bastian protests as the wind attempts to rip away his cloak.

The flags are snapping in the wind and threaten to overwhelm his voice.

"I think that he does," I reply. "This storm be his work." He truly is powerful if he can summon up such a storm at his bidding. "But surely its fierceness will hinder his army as much as it does us. I cannot see how this will aid in his attack."

Another lightning bolt lances across the heavens.

* * *

I hasten into the dungeons, built into the hill upon which the Keep stands tall. "Speak, D'Erlette, and tell of what thou know of Ulric's plans!" Only one cell from the half dozen small rooms is currently being used, the man standing behind the iron bars which block the opening looks up as I throw open the door to the dungeon. The dungeons are a simple place; three rooms line a short corridor dug from the hill. Iron bars bar each cell, and a stout door seals the hallway from the rest of the Keep.

"What need I say to thee?" the Count asks back haughtily. "I be noble born, of good Christian stock, unlike thee!"

"Thou might wish to reconsider thy position now that thou has had days to think upon thy fortunes." The cells are not damp, nor do the Harfleurs short their prisoner's rations. In the torchlight, I can see a small tray at the Count's feet, still bearing an empty soup bowl, half a bread loaf, and a flagon of water.

"He be of little use to us," Livia said as she glides out of the shadows.

D'Erlette starts at her words. He had failed to notice her arrival—small wonder given the aura which surrounds my own appearance. I have managed to draw essence from the tempest itself, wreathing myself in spectral lightning, before storming through the corridors of the Keep and barging into the dungeon.

Nor had I witnessed her following me, for that matter. Not a small thing either, for these deep corridors are all but deserted this night.

"Do not seek aid," she tells him as he opens his mouth, either to mock her or else to cry out for guards. "Thy guards are at the village walls standing firm against the Norsemen. Thou be alone...with us." She smiles then, baring her teeth at him in a manner that gives even me a momentary pause.

"Thou be all alone, where no man might hear thy screams."

D'Erlette looks around nervously at the iron bars that separate him from us. "Another demon?

It seems that Bastian consorts openly with the very dregs of the Christian Hell which he claims to despise so much!" He seems to draw comfort from his secure prison. "The Witch King will save me from thy foul powers," he tells us boldly. "He will set me free from these bars and I will take my place as overlord of this land."

"The Witch King? Ulric?" Livia laughs, a mocking sound echoed by a boom of thunder that shakes the very stones under our feet. "He will be lucky to save himself from us," she sneers. "Franc has slain how many of his men already? And with little effort too."

"I have strode into the very heart of Ulric's camp twice now and I have returned both times unharmed to tell the tale of my journey."

"It will not save thee. Thy powers will falter beneath the glory that is Ulric, the Witch King!"

"Mayhap, Richard, thy men will speak more readily than thou. I find that Livia can entice any man to speak all that he knows to her."

She smiles and idly entwines a strand of black hair around her pale-skinned finger. "'Tis true...men be simple creatures to manipulate." Her eyes seem to glow. "No mortal can resist my charms." The dress seems to fit more snugly around her bosom, though I know not how its cut could have changed so suddenly. "Surely thou would prefer to seek redemption and speak to us now of thy knowledge of Ulric's plots?"

"Keep silent and I cannot promise to control her for long," I add. "Her hungers are things of legend."

Livia licks her full lips, offering us both a smile.

D'Erlette shakes his head. "Do not tempt me, demons!" he snarls. "Get thee behind me!"

A bell tolls loudly, above the pealing thunder, signaling that another attack is underway despite the fiercely raging storm.

"We shall see who be right and who be wrong," D'Erlette tells us with a smile. Despite being behind the dungeon bars, he stands as tall and as proud as a king.

That smile bothers me. He should not be so confident.

Chapter Three

"The Norsemen are striking at us," Bastian tells me as I join him on the upper parapet of the Keep's southern wall. Rain drips from the cowl of his cloak as he stands and stares into the still-raging storm.

"How many and where?" I ask over a peal of thunder. Despite my sprint from the dungeons to the parapet, I am not winded in the slightest. My friend does not notice.

"They strike at a dozen or so different places along the wall. The ditch is slowing them and keeping most of them at a distance."

"The ditch be filling with water," Jacques tells us as he wipes water from his face. "Twill be a moat ere morning. A proper stream methinks."

"An added defense against fire then." I smile at that jest, for in this storm no fire could possibly burn for long. Even Ulric's three ritual-spawned bonfires have long since been extinguished. "In case lightning strikes." I feel a need to try and dispel some of the tension among the garrison. The storm has been fiercely raging for hours, and even now as midnight approaches, it shows no signs of slackening.

Nor do the Norsemen. They approach the palisade, loosen some arrows and shout curses at us, and then withdraw into the storm. They have been doing such for hours.

"Perhaps they seek to tire us, wear us down before they strike for real."

"They also tire themselves," Bastian points out.

"Mayhap they feed off Ulric's magick."

I consider that possibility, but dismiss it with a quick shake of my head. "'Tis more likely that he knows of some herb or potion which might sustain the fury of his men for a long time," I admit, "but sadly I know not of any such herb in our own stores." Mayhap I should have tried to find some of that potion he had promised to Sven for our own use...but no doubt such a draught would be cursed and tainted.

"Would the Lady Livia know of such?"

I shake my head at that question. "I do not know." Often she has surprised me with the wide variety of knowledge she possesses.

"Jacques, seek the Lady out and inquire if she possesses such knowledge. The storm and the feints are tiring us. If we can counteract our weariness with a simple herbal draft, then I would offer up a desire to sip it first for myself."

"I would be wary of making such a rash boast, Bastian. As thy father will no doubt attest, most herbal draughts often lack a sweet taste." I smile. "Indeed, I often think that the healers themselves add a little extra to make the taste just a bit more memorable."

Bastian smiles back at me. "Aye, I have heard him complain repeatedly upon that very subject."

"The rain is also affecting the quality of our bowstrings." Jacques pulls his cloak further forward to shield his face from the blowing rain. "The bowmen have given up trying to keep their strings dry and protected from the rain, my Lord. We have all but ceased using arrows."

"Not that the shafts will fly true in this wind and rain," I add.

"The only mercy of this truth be the fact that the Norsemen themselves are also unable to wield bows now. Or at least those they do use be few in number and limited in range."

"'Tis true, Jacques, but there naught that we can do." I gesture towards the tower of the Keep.

"I believe that Livia is spending time this night with Charles. Seek her there first...if she be not there, then mayhap Charles will know where she lurks."

"Aye." Jacques bows his head to Bastian and then hurries into the Keep proper.

"I envy my father his warm bed this night."

"I spoke with him earlier. He envies thou for thy ability to be out here in the storm and facing the foe from thy own walls."

Bastian smiles weakly.

"We shall fight well. Thy men have no thought of surrender."

"I know." Thunder rumbles in the distance while Bastian stares towards the distant Norse camp. "Can thou see the wizard?" he asks me.

"See him?"

"Aye. Thou are not a mortal man, Franc, and thou and I both know this." The two closest men-at-arms are too distant to hear our words. "Thou have powers, whether a blessing from God or a curse from the Devil I know not. Nor do I find that I care overmuch whichever it might be for thou have chosen to use thy powers and talents in the defense of my family and home and people."

I feel the unaccustomed warmth of a blush in my cheeks. "I thank ye."

"So, can thou see him?"

"Hmm." I squint into the storm. "I think that I can!" My eyes narrow, trying to see a certain figure more clearly. The damned rain and darkness are bothersome even to me. Surely Bastian and most of his men-at-arms can see naught at all at this distance.

If that that black-robed figure is indeed him, then he is speaking with one small group of Norsemen and gesturing towards the village as he does so. I cannot hear his speech, not at this distance and certainly not over the wrath of the storm, but I can make a guess at his words.

Attack.

"Ah, for a bow!" Bastian mutters.

"Aye," I agree.

More Norsemen charge the wall to our left and I hear shouts from the garrison as they rally to try and slay a few of the attackers with arrows.

"'Tis not enough," I mutter as the bowmen loose their shafts and a few Norsemen fall to their arrows.

"A sortie then?"

"Nay, Bastian, for that will only weaken our strength within these walls. The time is not yet right for us to sally forth and engage them in hand-to-hand before the walls of thy home." I place a hand on his shoulder. "But such a time is drawing close."

The night is passing, slowly. I know not how many hours have been spent in pacing along the parapet, but I suspect that the number is high. Bastian seems tireless in his pacing. The rain has slackened somewhat, but it has done so before and then fell again with its former ferocity.

"Thou should drink more tea," I tell him. "Or mulled wine or cider. Something hot to keep back the night's chill and the dampness."

"I don't feel cold."

"Thou are warmed by thy anger."

"Aye, and what of it?" Bastian wipes rain from his face. "My home is under near constant attack. The Norsemen have been probing at us all night."

"Aye." A bright bolt of lightning flashes overhead, sending shadows dancing.

A fresh volley of shouts and cries rises over the booming thunder.

"More of them are striking at us!"

I look at Bastian and nod. "No less than five separate locations this time." I have taken careful note and counts during the flashes of lightning.

"Spaced along the palisade to spread out my soldiers." Bastian tightens his grip on his sword and returns to his pacing. "We must respond to this, but how? If we concentrate ourselves to much, then we leave the rest of wall vulnerable."

"Aye. But the moat will slow the advance of the Norsemen." I pause for a moment, mentally feeling the tempo of the storm. "Rally thy reserves. Send every man and boy who might draw a bow or wield an axe or sword to the wall."

Bastian freezes in mid-step. "Then thou think that it is time?"

"Aye." That single word still conveys the chill in my voice. "He is out there and they are coming."

"To arms," Bastian snaps at one of his retainers and the man scurries from the parapet. "Blow the horns and summon the men to the square." He looks at me with a pleased expression upon his face.

"At last we shall smite the Norsemen with our steel."

"I trust that thy steel shall prove a match to their wrath." I turn my eyes back to the south. The storm has slackened enough that I hope to be able to see the Norse camp. I can make out the tents, but not any faces on the handful of figures I see moving amongst them. "I do not see Ulric anywhere."

"Mayhap we should move to the palisade." Bastian is staring towards the sounds of battle.

"Aye, such a move would now be wise. Our lofty vantage will no longer serve our needs. 'Tis now time for bared steel."

"Cum Saxum Saxorum," Ulric's voice rises on the wind. "Induersum montum oparium da—"

"Where is the cursed man?" I snarl. I can hear him so clearly, but he is invisible to my eyes!

"—in Aetibulum.,"

"He sounds so close."

"Aye, Bastian." I feel a chill strike me, and not from the night rain. "By all the gods!" He could not be here! "At the wall!"

"In Quintum," Ulric's voice grows to a shout, "Draconis!"

With a tremendous and earth-shattering roar, lightning strikes at the palisade. A large section of the wooden wall vanishes into a swirling yellowish mist.

Throughout the village, men fall silent in wonderment and in terror.

"Do the gods themselves fight on the Witch King's side?" Bastian calls to me as wisps of foul-smelling mist are sent billowing over us in the gusting wind. I hear coughing from our guards. "The entire town is shrouded by that sulphurous cloud."

"'Twas Dragon's Bane," I curse as the mist clears. At least the blowing wind is good for something. "Apparently Ulric also knows of its power and the spell of its making." Not something I had expected.

The rain slackens away almost to nothing in a moment and I peer towards the palisade trying to assess the damage.

A portion of the log wall has been ripped asunder by the blast. And now Norseman are pouring through the gaping hole, axes and spears brandished in waving arms, their voices raised in a shrill cry.

"They fight like animals!" Bastian curses as he sees several of his men closest to the breach cut down like autumn wheat before the invaders.

"Some foul potion of Ulric's twisting their minds no doubt." Their rage cannot be natural! It cannot be.

Bastian whirls away from the parapet. "We must take arms up now! They'll burn the village down around us." He hurries down the stairs to the ground, his men-at-arms following at his heels.

"Too arms!" I hear him call from within the Keep. "To the wall!"

"To the wall." I jump from the parapet to the ground, bending my knees as I land to cushion the fall. A much softer landing than when I had jumped from the tower to save Bastian. "Aye, to the breach methinks!" I check my sword and hasten through the once again pouring rain towards the palisade.

Chapter Four

Fresh lightning bolts flash overhead, this time striking at some unfortunate tree in the nearby forest. The chill wind suddenly gusts fiercely and blows cold rain into the shadows where I stand, forcing me to clutch my cloak more tightly around me. Not because I am cold, but because the sound of flapping cloth might give me away to other watchers in the night. I stare wide-eyed at the breached palisade.

The wall itself stretches to the cliffs, beyond my sight, but less than twenty paces from where I sand and wait, the logs gape brokenly. The breach is a good twelve paces wide. The logs in the centre are missing entirely and many of the ones closer to where the wall still stands intact are now broken off jaggedly a pace or so from the ground. Wisps of smoke are still curling from a few of the broken logs, despite the rain.

A strong stench still hangs in the air, harsh and choking. Sulfur from the Dragon's Bane no doubt.

The clang of metal against metal echoes from a few streets over, but I have avoided the spot.

Let Bastian and his retainers fight there, I know that I will be needed elsewhere.

There are still Norsemen attacking other parts of the wall. I took note of the sounds of battle as I made my way through the town. The streets had proven to be more crowded than I had expected to find. The sounds and excitement of the early evening ritual and the later growing battle had kept many of the townsfolk awake. The explosion of the Dragon's Bane had awakened those who did slumber and sent scores of families into the streets, most fleeing towards the Keep. Between them and the men-at-arms hurrying hither and thither, the night has become a scene of chaos.

A chaos which might either help or hinder Ulric and Bastian both. The chaos will divert some of Bastian's men into crowd control; it will also distract the Norsemen from rapidly securing the town.

Footsteps echo in the dark and my eyes flick towards the nearest corner. Half a dozen of Bastian's men-at-arms are hurrying towards the breach. Two of them carry spluttering torches. The leader begins to point his men into positions of his choosing. "We need to block this gap before more of the savages gain entrance to the town."

"Aye, Captain."

"God alone knows how long Lord Harfleur can hold them back. We need this wall fixed." He rests his hand on his sheathed sword. "Stand fast, men. Reinforcements and craftsmen will arrive soon. It will fall upon our shoulders to hold back the barbarians while repairs are made."

I can only see temporary repairs being made while storm and battle both rage, and temporary repairs will not serve to hold back the Norsemen for long. Not with Ulric desperate to gain access to the Keep. A soft grunt draws my eyes to the gap in the palisade.

Two big brutish Norsemen step through the broken logs, carrying axes with shafts as long as my arms and as thick around as my thighs. They pause for a moment to stare coldly at the town guards who nervously grip their own weapons.

Good odds, I think, and then Ulric steps through the gap, followed by a number of men in roughly-woven black tunics and cloaks. Several of them carry torches of their own, spluttering in the wind and rain.

Even the storm seems to pause a moment at the tableau.

"Kill them," Ulric orders with a dismissive wave of his hand and his two brutes lunge forward to obey.

"Have at ye!" one of the men-at-arms shouts and swings his sword at the man on the left. His companions cast aside their torches and hasten to draw their own swords.

The two Norsemen fight like animals, striking down the guards with violent strokes of their axes. They do not try to avoid any of the counterblows, but still very few cuts mar either their clothing or skin.

Something is wrong with them...very wrong.

The two brutes hack the last man down and leave him laying in the mud in a slowly spreading pool of his own blood. I lick my lips as I stare at it. Precious blood....

"The scroll is what I seek here!" Ulric hisses to several of his hooded minions who have followed him through the hole in the wall. "We storm the Keep! Find the library and fetch me the scrolls therein."

"Which scroll, Master?"

"All of them!" Ulric's eyes blaze. "Bring all of them, fool, if thou must!" He gestures to the distant Keep. "It lays within those walls...I can feel it." He sounds like a man lost in rapture. "I can feel it!" he repeats. Drawing his cloak about him, he strides towards the Keep even as more of his rabid followers hurry through the broken palisade and scatter into the dark village leaving the street deserted.

I look around hastily. Barrels, several fallen and a few broken from the force of the Dragon's Bane. A wagon stands near one house. Broken timber from the palisade, mostly too small to be of use for ought other than kindling a fire.

A hay-wain is not much. But it will do. It will do nicely methinks. I hurriedly stride to the wain and begin to push. It will have to do. 'Tis hard going, for the wain proves heavier than I had thought at first, but with a great effort I manage to push the wain in front of the gap in the palisade to stop other Norsemen from gaining entrance. I smash the axle with my sword and break loose the wheels to further slow any attempts at moving it. I hope that it will be enough.

Then I hurry back into the village. I am needed....

* * *

A shrill scream breaks the stillness.

Slipping from the shadows, like the very demon I have been called in the past, I strike at one Norseman and wince as his life's blood pours onto the ground, wasted. The peasant woman he has cornered against the wall of a short alleyway stares at us both as if we have sprouted horns and dragon wings and I hastily seek to comfort her with a few gentle words. But then the Norseman's companion comes at me.

He bears neither sword nor axe and he has discarded his tunic and torn at his breeches as an animal might claw at a bag confining it. He is tall and blond and built like an oak tree. Handsome mayhap, but right now his face is contorted into a feral snarl, flecks of foam dripping from his open mouth as he stares at me with burning eyes. He is panting. He is more animal than man, berserk with rage and his mind almost certainly addled by one of Ulric's foul potions.

I seek to strike him down with a swift blow from my sword, put him out of his misery, but he slips under my swing and seizes me in his arms.

At that, I almost laugh at the notion that this mortal seeks to harm me in such a physical way, but then the first chuckles of my laughter turn to silence as his grip tightens.

I actually feel my ribs groan.

He is stronger than an ox, enraged like a bear.

Shadow's Kiss has fallen from my fingers, splashing uselessly into a puddle. My hands grasp at his arms and try to break his own grip upon me. It is a serious challenge, but slowly—ever so slowly—I force his deadly hug to loosen and then I break free. I hear myself grunting in anger and effort. I give in to my darker nature then, calling upon my own reserves of strength and skill to break completely free. My eyes burn and my lips curl into a snarl. Now it is my turn to strike and my pale hands wrap around his arms, pressing them to his side while I move my head in close. He smells wrong, like a rapid animal.

He tries to bite me, snarling like a wild beast.

"Not like that foolish mortal...let me show how 'tis properly done." I lean in closer and sink my fangs into his neck. The taste of his blood fills my mouth.

Salty.

Fiery...something burns.

His essence is rich, like liquid flame.

It fills me, warming me, and then it boils within my stomach, through my veins. It is raw power, strength and invincibility coursing within me.

I let him go and he collapses bonelessly onto the muddy ground. I pant, bent over, seeking to find myself again. I had almost became lost within my own bloodlust...almost became an animal. Like him.

And yet, it had been nice.

It had been oddly refreshing, to give in like that. Mayhap it has been too long since I surrendered to my baser nature. It had been vitally necessary for only an animal could triumph against such odds as those I now faced.

Suddenly I remember the woman whom I have tried to save.

The peasant woman has vanished while we struggled. I cannot blame her.

Lightning flashes across the sky, casting the town into frozen moments with each burst of light.

The streets echo to the sound of my booted feet as I run.

Passing by a group of men-at-arms squaring off against an equal number of Norsemen. They are well-trained and competent men so I see little need to linger here. Urgent needs fills my mind, calling me towards the Keep though I cannot say why I am needed back there.

Rounding a corner, I observe a Norseman sprawled in the mud with an arrow sticking from his chest. No sign of the archer.

A few flames sullenly burn in the open doorway of a cottage. The family appears to have fled and in this rain, the fire cannot gain hold.

Still lightning flashes overhead and the rumble of thunder is mixed with the sounds of battle.

Somewhere in this town is Ulric. Somehow I must find him. I must kill him.

Another corner brings me face-to-face with an unexpected, though pleasant sight. Three of D'Erlette's men-at-arms are crossing swords with two of Ulric's berserkers. 'Crossing swords' might be a trifle ill-stated though, for neither of Ulric's men carry any weapons though they fight like feral beasts. The scent of wrongness hangs around them as well.

It must be a potion of some kind!

I can think of no other cause that would give the scent of wrongness, nor addle mens' minds into behaving like beasts.

One of the men-at-arms falls, his unarmed foe clawing at his eyes. Another man-at-arms lays dead, whilst the third is slowly backing away from the snarling Norseman.

"I have no time for this!" I snap in frustration. "Must I do everything myself?" I slash through the neck of the crouching berserker. Ignoring the sobbing of the man laying under the headless corpse, I turn to the other Norseman as he lunges at me. I punch him. Hard.

He barely seems fazed though my blow should have knocked him senseless. He bears his teeth at me and leaps at me with a shriek.

Shadow's Kiss slices through his neck.

"Aid thy companion," I tell the remaining man-at-arms. "I am needed elsewhere."

And something draws me ever towards the Keep. Something calls me with the faintest scent of must in the night air.

Chapter Five

The gates of the Keep gape open and light from the torches within spills out onto the muddy ground before them.

A dozen Harfleur men-at-arms lay on the ground, dead. Their blood is already cold. I can smell it on the night air. Sour. Nearly twice that number of Norsemen litter the ground as well. Ulric's brutes, and one or two who have the look of clerics or war chieftains among them. All of the bodies bear marks of violence...hacked by axes and cut by swords, and several of Ulric's minions have been slain by arrows.

No sign of Ulric himself, worse luck.

I hastily look up at the battlements as lightning lances between the clouds once again, but they are empty of archers or other guards. The clang of swords echoes from within the Keep however, showing that even here men fight and die.

"Damn." The gates are open, breached. The stone walls are intact and even the wooden slats of the open gates are firm and yet the Keep has been penetrated. Treachery perhaps?

Rain blows into my face but I ignore the drops.

The blood of the fallen is being washed away, wasted, but I can still smell it. I can still hunger for it, despite knowing that it is now cold and sour and rancid. I grow hungry....

I turn to stare down at the village, straining to determine events through the still-pouring rain. I can see torches flickering, though whether being carried by friend or foe I cannot say. A handful of houses or shops have been set ablaze, though the rain is helping to contain the fires. I can even see some of the Norse corpses on the road which forewarned me that the Keep had been attacked directly.

My hand tightens upon my sword. "What must I do?" I call into the storm. "Battle below and battle here. I feel torn in twain!"

A woman's scream rings out from within the Keep.

My choice is made for me. I hasten into the Keep, my boots thudding on the stones.

The library of Keep Harfleur is a fairly small room, its floor crammed with three desks and its walls covered with many shelves of rolled up scrolls and not a few hand-copied books. Precious things, those books, and a true treasure for the Harfleur family. Candles flicker in their wall sconces and in stands on the desks, but the room itself seems untouched by the violence which has torn apart the town.

After a momentary pause, I step into it and look around carefully. My hearing is attuned to the slightest sound and yet I hear nothing. Nothing from the room that is, for I can hear the clash of steel and the cries of men elsewhere in the Keep. I sheath my sword. Shadow's Kiss has served me well this night, and has tasted the blood of a score or more. Most likely more, though I failed to keep count. I have avenged the fallen defenders of the Keep, slain the enemy as I came upon them, though it still does not be enough.

I must stop Ulric.

And I must prevent him from gaining the prize that he seeks and values so highly.

Where can the scroll be that he so covets?

Aside from the rolled up scrolls, only a few candles and two or three pottery urns line the shelves.

My nose wrinkles at a hint of a strong musty smell. "What scroll does he search for?" I glance through some of the scrolls abandoned on the nearest desk, and then discard them to move deeper into the room. "Bibles and prayers, treatises on herbs, records of the land and its people, so many scrolls."

I can be here for days searching and I know not what it is that I seek!

With a sudden snarl of anger, I thump my fist against one of the shelf-covered walls and an urn atop it topples to the floor. The urn shatters.

There amid the broken pottery is a rolled up scroll.

A hidden scroll.

I carefully pick it up. It is old, the parchment dry and cracking even in my gentle grip. The ribbon holding it rolled is faded and crumbles away as I pick it up.

"Well done, Man of Gaul. I applaud thy efforts. Truly I do."

I turn towards Ulric as he emerges from the shadows near the open door, his black cloak pulling shadows more tightly around him. "Thou do be persistent, Witch King." My hand drifts to my sword hilt, but I do not yet unsheathe Shadow's Kiss. My nose wrinkles—the musty smell emanates from Ulric. The smell is more than simple must, methinks. 'Tis the stench of decay.

"I have had long years to practice and prepare, Demonspawn. Long years of searching the wide world for a particular scroll." His gnarled hands twitch, claw-like. "I suggest that thou turn over the scroll to me...what can it be worth to thee?"

Faces flash before my eyes, past and present. "The lives of friends?" I can see them so clearly in my head, as if they stand at my side even now. "Myrddin. My friends in Paris. How many others have thou slain whom I do not know?"

His dark green eyes narrow at my accusation. "They were nothing," he tells me with a dismissive wave of his left hand. "An annoyance to be swept aside whilst I seek out the scroll."

"Perhaps I feel differently then." I hold the scroll near a flickering candle. "Perhaps this roll of parchment can also be swept aside." I take pleasure at tossing his words back into his face.

His eyes are locked onto the scroll as its end dips precariously near the candle flame.

"So what is it?" I ask him.

Perhaps the tone of my voice—cold and harder than a winter blizzard—convinces him to be honest with me. Perhaps he merely thinks to toy with me. In any event, a small smile twists his cracked lips.

"'Tis but the key to a small treasure...but what is treasure to one of thy Kind?" he counters dismissively. "'Tis of no importance to thee surely." He holds out his right hand. "Give it to me."

"No."

"Give it to me or suffer!" he snarls at me, his eyes burning with venomous hatred. "I must have that scroll!"

I touch the end to the candle and watch as eager flames ravenously begin to devour the parchment.

"No!" Ulric screams and throws himself at me.

I drop the scroll to the stone floor and raise a hand to strike him aside.

He strikes me first, hard, and knocks me to the floor. I am aghast—no mortal should possess such strength! Not even his potion-crazed Berserkers possess such raw strength. And the look of rage in his eyes had given even me pause. Shaking off my surprise, I smoothly rise to my feet and take a step forward.

Ulric has snatched the scroll from the floor and extinguished the fire before all of the parchment has been consumed. Now he turns on me with a snarl worthy of a wild beast. His eyes blaze with unholy rage as he lunges again at me. His hand strikes against my face even as I slap him...I could topple a strong blacksmith with a single blow but the old man seems merely startled.

As am I. That blow should have snapped his neck like a dried out twig! Even as I prepare to strike again, harder this time, he punches me and I am knocked back against the wall. Slamming into a row of shelves, I slump to the floor, stunned. A few scrolls fall from their shelves to land atop me.

With my fall, the rage seems to flow out of Ulric and he stares down at me with what looks to be sadness in his green eyes. "Thou do not understand," he tells me calmly, once again appearing to be a harmless old greybeard. "I have waited decades for this scroll to come into my possession. I will not allow thy actions to thwart me now." He looks down at the roll of parchment clenched in his hand. His knuckles are white with his grip. "I will gain control of the talisman and then gain dominion over all of the world!"

"Who wants to rule the world?" I croak in a weak voice. "All those mortals whining about their problems? Scroll work. Bureaucracy. Too much bother really." I try to move but my limbs feel like lead.

"Silence, creature." He smiles dreamily at me. "The talisman will make me powerful enough to challenge Odin himself! I will overthrow the Allfather and rule all of Midgard!"

"I think not," a man-at-arms says as he steps through the doorway, a drawn sword in his hand.

"Don't move, Norseman!"

I open my mouth to warn the man, but no sounds emerge from my lips.

The Witch King turns and casually plucks the sword from the startled man-at-arm's fingers. "I have no time for thee." He rams the sword into the unfortunate man's chest and then drops the now-limp body as if it is nothing more than a dirty tunic. "I will have a later use for thee, creature, for thy blood will be an important part of the ritual I must yet conduct."

The scent of blood from the slain guard is intoxicating, overwhelming the stench of must emanating from Ulric.

"The talisman is almost mine."

I can feel myself starting to drool...all this exertion tonight has made me hungry, despite my earlier feeding. Or mayhap 'tis because of the potion within the berserker's veins? So very hungry!

Even the scent of rapidly cooling blood, growing sour on the floor, is twisting at my self-control.

Ulric chuckles, swaying on his feet. "After so long it is within my grasp. So very long...."

He appears to have forgotten about me. I lunge to my feet with all the non-Human swiftness I can muster. Despite my unsteadiness, I cross the space that separates us in just two strides and seize him in my grasp. "And thy blood," I tell him gleefully, "will be most refreshing." I sink my fangs into his neck and begin to feed.

Ulric struggles, desperately, but it avails him not for now he is within my power and without tricks and magicks to cast. I shiver as his strength flows into me.

He murmurs, incoherent in his panic, and struggles desperately. His punches and kicks are half-hearted and poorly aimed and I ignore them just as I would ignore a mosquito on my boot.

I drain him, enjoying every instant of it, for his essence is rich and vital. A veritable feast.

Chapter Six

"Thou live?" Bastian asks from the library doorway.

"Aye. Sorry to disappoint ye."

He winces at the mocking tone of my voice and takes a step into the room. "I meant that not as it sounded, Franc. Keep Harfleur is deep within thy debt on this day. Without thy aide, my father's land would have been swept away by the Norseman and all would now be lost." His eyes come to rest on the fallen corpse of Ulric. He half draws his sword before realizing that Ulric's chest does not rise nor fall. He looks at me.

"The devil himself," I agree with his unspoken question. "Slain by my own hand."

"Again we are in thy debt." Bastian looks tired, worn from the night's battle, and the long days-long siege. He sways slightly even as he offers me a polite bow.

"'Twas nothing...he annoyed me and thus I take pride in his death." I look down at the shriveled body and lick my lips. His essence had been delectable...strong and sharp and wonderful.

Even as the blood cooled and his essence soured, he had remained tasty. I wish to dine upon him again and again, but sadly he is already drained.

"Guards, remove this trash." Bastian steps aside to allow to two of his retainers to lift Ulric's body from where it sprawls, and carry it from the room.

"The battle is won then?" I ask. The Keep has fallen silent at least as far as battle is concerned.

I can detect no sounds of fighting, no crossing of swords echoing through the corridors. I do hear distant moans from wounded men still laying in those places where they fell. I wonder at the sense of silence, then realize that the storm has lessened and thunder no longer shakes the stones of the Keep.

"The Norsemen are fleeing," Livia announces as she glides into the room. "As if they know that the battle is lost and their king is slain." She glances back over her shoulder. "Even the gods-accursed storm is abating at last." She is still looking radiant, without any visible evidence of the night's turmoil marring either her clothing or hair...and yet I can smell the faintest hint of blood about her. Her radiance is even more apparent to me, knowing that she has fed this night.

"Thou have spent the night in safety, Livia?"

"Aye, Franc. I avoided the chaos of the outer walls and remained within the Keep." She quickly glances over at Bastian, but the young nobleman seems absorbed by the place where the body of his hated foe had lain. "I took shelter with Lord Harfleur, at his invitation, and sat at his window to tell him what I could see of the battle as it progressed. He was most intrigued by my tales of how the Norsemen broke through the palisade. I saw thee leap from the parapet, but felt little need to mention that in my tale. As the Norsemen fought their way to the gates of the Keep, I prepared herbs for Charles to drink in his wine. He slumbers even now."

"I thank thee."

"The foolish old man would have been calling for his sword and his armor and attempting to fight the invaders from his sickbed. Nay, I could not bear to see him thus."

I can only frown at her. Is she softening? As well to ask the winter to be less chill than Livia to become soft-hearted.

"After he slumbered, I calmed the healers and sent some forth to aid the wounded. With guards, I might add. The battle in the halls was brutal, yet thy friends prevailed. I even found time to sup briefly." Her smile is wide, her expression as pleased as a recently fed kitten.

"I trust that thy meal was to thy liking." I can only hope that it was some Norseman and not one of the Keep's servants or guards.

She winks at me and licks her moist lips.

"And so it is over then and the Norsemen flee?"

"Aye," Bastian nods. "They flee, but we do not pursue though. I will not waste men in further battle this night. Let them slink back to their ships and sail away home."

"A noble sentiment," I tell him. He has a spill of blood splashed across his chest and arms. Not his own, though for he moves without a trace of injury.

"But Franc, how did thou come to find the Witch King? The confusion of the battle lay thick upon us all. I was in the town when word came that the foe laid siege to the Keep's very walls. I rallied what men I could and returned hither and found the gates open." His expression darkens.

"'Twas treachery by a handful of D'Erlette's own men-at-arms. They were slain by my retainers and the last of them fell to the same Norsemen they helped enter the Keep."

Again the worm of treachery burrows into the heart of men. "I overheard Ulric talking to some of his minions as they entered the town. I had just finishing slaying several of the foe near the breach in the palisade and was lurking close enough to listen to his words." A modest enough feat after all.

"One questioned his purpose and he replied that he sought some ancient scroll."

Bastian starts.

"A scroll?" Livia asks. "A scroll?" Her voice rises sharply with the repetition and the disbelief which colours her tone is mirrored by her wide-eyed expression. "He launched an invasion and a small war over some silly piece of parchment!"

"Apparently."

Livia snorts loudly. "The foolishness of men ceases not to amaze me." She shakes her head and mutters under her breath.

"Art thou finished?" I ask politely. I only caught a fraction of her muttering, but none of those words were the least bit ladylike nor demure.

For a long moment she stares at me with her cold green eyes, but then at last she nods. "Aye, for now." She looks around the library. "There be many scrolls here."

"Some hidden," I say, glancing briefly at the broken urn. "What do thou know of hidden scrolls, Bastian Harfleur?" My eyes lock with his.

He starts and his hand tightens on his sword hilt for a moment.

Livia looks at him, narrowing her own eyes.

The seconds stretch out in a rather uncomfortable silence.

"I know of one mysterious scroll that mayhap be the one which thou speak of. The one that Ulric covets so much." He pauses for a moment, as if coming to some difficult decision. "It is an old scroll." He walks over to one of the desks, the one farthest from the door, and bends down to loosen the back leg. Still stooping, he reaches into the compartment thus revealed and withdraws a tightly rolled scroll. "'Tis very valuable. Ancient and treasured by my family for years beyond count." He unrolls the parchment with great care and then hands it to me.

I look at the scroll. "Something is written here." The ink is faded with age, some letters missing entirely, but enough remains that I think I can puzzle it out.

"'Tis very old," Bastian reminds us both. "'Twas first brought to these lands by my greatfather's greatfather."

"Did he pen these words himself?"

"Nay, Franc. At least, not that he ever told a living soul."

"I see."

"What is it?" Livia asks me. "What does it say?" She moves closer to my side and attempts to gain a peek at the writing.

"'Tis old indeed. A form of Latin script that was archaic even in Rome's youth." It is almost certainly older than myself. "Mayhap older even than Rome," I whisper.

Livia hears me, but Bastian does not. Her eyes widen in surprise. She looks anew at the parchment and her expression grows thoughtful.

"Can thou read it?" Bastian asks. "My father showed me the scroll once, before we did hide it away, but he did not know the script. If the meaning was indeed to my ancestors, then it has been lost over the years."

"I have some passing knowledge of the words herein," I tell him as I study the faded ink once again. "The penmanship is poor, and the ink faded with the passage of years, yet I think I can make out enough to gather the intent." I pause, holding the scroll so that it catches the light more readily.

"' Where gods and giants wage war which never ceased,
where the skies darken and ominous storm clouds churn, that Talisman which does give life to those deceased, be hidden within the desolation of the Wyrm.
For those men who be sufficiently bold,
it rests in the darkness far beneath,
in the once-fiery heart, now dark and cold,
under the jagged peaks of the Frost Giant's teeth. '"

"There are other lines penned here which I cannot read...'tis a tongue completely unknown to me." I shake my head. "This seems like a warning of sorts."

"A prophecy. Mayhap a guide to a great treasure." Bastian pauses. "A Talisman of sorts."

"Aye, but what kind of magic does it use."

Livia looks over my shoulder. "By the gods," she whispers softly.

I look at her sharply. She seems even paler than usual. "What is it?" I ask her. "Can thou read those lines?"

"Aye, and truly do I wish that I could not." She shivers. "'Tis not a pleasing script, and not meant for human mouths to speak, nor for human ears to hear methinks."

"Read them," Bastian orders. "Tell us all that this scroll do say. Please," he adds after a moment.

"' That which be not yet dead will eternal lie, and with long years, even Death might one day die.'" Livia's voice echoes hollowly through the library. She has quoted the phrase perfectly from memory without bothering to read from the scroll as I did, speaking in a tired voice devoid of passion or emotion. And the room feels chilled now. "Those are old words," she tells us, looking away from us, her eyes glazing as she stares off into unknown distances and places. "Ancient when even the earth was young."

Bastian shakes his head. "But what does it mean?" he asks.

"Now that is indeed the mystery," I tell him in a soft voice.

Chapter Seven

"'Twas brought by our family from the Norselands," Charles Harfleur tells us in a tired voice.

"Brought to us from the harsh lands of the frost giants and the fierce warrior gods."

Bastian stands by his father's bedside, while Livia and I stand at the foot of the bed. Charles is pale and well-wrapped in blankets with a fire burning in the hearth, and yet he is wide awake and alert.

He has summoned us to his chambers and demanded the tally of the battle—the numbers of dead and injured on both sides, the prisoners taken, the condition of the nearby farms and of the village and his Keep. The healers had protested, of course, and yet he has mustered strength enough to override their complaints and order them from his bedside.

"This will help him sleep and heal." Livia finishes mixing a whitish powder into a small goblet of mulled wine and hands it to Bastian who holds the goblet steady while his father drinks. "'Tis a simple powdered herb mix of my own grinding and blending."

Bastian nods his thanks to her.

"The same herbal mix I served him last night," she tells me.

"The Norsemen believe in this Talisman...an implement of great magic known throughout the world," Charles continues after his drink. He does not seem to notice the herbs added to his wine.

"The Celts, the Gauls, the Norsemen, the Greeks and Romans, the Egyptians, and mayhap even the Chin and the Songs might know of it by some local legend."

"A talisman?" Livia asks. "What might it do?"

"It can resurrect the dead."

I stare at Livia as the simple statement sinks in.

"A magical device which gives life to the dead and makes the living immortal. A gift of the gods, or a curse from the very depths of hell."

Charles shakes his head weakly and leans back against his pillows. "I fear that such potent magic should not rest in the hands of mortal men. Better that such knowledge be lost in the mists of legend for all time."

"No, I can see thy point." Livia nods her head.

I notice her fingernails carving thin slivers of wood from the bed-frame where they grip it. She is agitated.

"But what else do thou know of this?"

"The scroll was given to my greatfather's father by one of the last druids in Britannia. My sire was serving in a Roman cohort and had helped to subdue the Celtic tribes there. The Celts came from the same stock as the Norsemen, even though they split asunder so long ago…"

Perhaps that was why Myrddin had been slain…perhaps Ulric had thought that Myrddin had possessed some secret knowledge of the scroll I now held in my hands.

"The Talisman must be found."

I look at Livia with a sharp glance, but I am the only one to catch her sudden smile as she speaks the words in a low tone. "Be thou certain of that?" I ask her. She had spoken up suddenly, seemingly certain of what she said.

"It is a potent artifact, if the legend be true," Bastian points out.

"Too potent," Charles counters. He leans back into his blankets and coughs weakly. "Such magic be too dangerous to possess. Better that such arts be lost forever in the passage of time."

"Yet with the scroll, perhaps it can be found anew. Not all who might seek it are corrupt. Not everyone will use its powers for ill." Livia looks at Bastian and flutters her eyelashes at him.

I sigh at the display.

Bastian is staring at her, his mouth half-open and his eyes glazed.

"In the right hands, it could be protected and any misuse prevented," Livia sounds quite reasonable in that assumption.

"Misuse will come about by its very nature!" Charles snaps and Bastian shakes his head guiltily.

"Ulric sought it while he lived…I wonder how many others know of this scroll? How many legends does this talisman exist within?"

"Even one be too many."

"I will journey north, methinks." I can scarcely believe the words that I speak even as my mouth opens and the sounds issue forth. "Either I will find this talisman or else I will prove the falseness of the legend."

Charles nods weakly. "If it be true, then thou must know caution, Franc. I counsel against such a course of action."

"I hear thy words, Charles, yet I must do this."

"The Norselands are not a place to be traveled lightly. The harshness of the land is matched by the weather and the fierce tempers of the natives."

"I can handle myself." I have little fear of what the north holds for me.

"I sense that nothing good will come of this. Thou meddle with things better left lost. The power of such a talisman will corrupt thee if thy soul be not strong and pure."

"I fear not its power. My soul be strong," I reply with a grin.

Charles looks at me with sadness—even a hint of pity—in his eyes. "I can only hope so," he says. "For the sake of the world."

* * *

Alone in my chambers, I stare down at the stones in my hand. Three small river-rounded stones. Dawn, Dusk, and Midnight. One gold, one silver, and one black. They seem to glow in the light of the sole candle that burns on the small table.

The Triscale Stones.

I am unsure of how long I have stood there, just looking at them. Such a silly thing really, to try and plan my life according to the fall of some mere stones…and yet I have felt restless until I returned to my chambers and tipped the stones from my belt pouch into my hand. I have never had much affinity for magick of any kind, not until recently, and yet I feel a power swelling deep within me.

"Should I journey north in search of this talisman?" I finally ask aloud and toss the stones onto the floor.

They roll and clink softly across it.

The black stone is touching the gold one. The silver stone has rolled clear to the wall, as far away from the others as it can be and still be within the room. Midnight marks out the Dawn as its mate and Dusk is cast aside.

The answer to my query is quite clearly Yes. I blow out the candle.

* * *

"I trust these steeds will serve thee well." The sun is bright overhead.

"Aye, Bastian. Tempest will sire many a fine foal for thy stables and these old horses of thine shall be fine." I pat the muzzle of my new black horse. "A fine steed like Tempest will not be required for long and I would grieve to lose him in some town whilst I take ship across the northern sea. Better that he lives here and enjoys the comfort of thy stables."

Livia glances at me once, and then nods in agreement. "I shall enjoy riding a steed of my own,"

she informs us, "for I grew weary of sharing a saddle with Franc on our last ride." She then lowers her voice so that only I, with my sharp hearing, might catch her words. "Even though I know not wither we journey." She pats the muzzle of her grey mare.

It has not been fun riding two to a horse, I agree silently. "Nightbreeze will carry you well," I say aloud. "She rescued Charles and galloped clear from the Norse camp." And she was a fine prize for Livia to ride.

"Ride well and good journey. Both I and my father will look forward to thy next visit here, Franc. Nevermore shall I name thee Stormcrow, for thou have proven to be a good friend and true."

"And thou have grown much and matured more in recent days. The people of the lands hereabouts will have a good lord to govern over them in the years to come."

"Yes." His eyes are gazing eastward now.

"Thou think of the future then?"

"The near future, my Lady. The eastern lands be rich and lack a ruler now that D'Erlette rests within our dungeons...mayhap I should journey there. With no strong local lord to govern and protect them, bandits and other villains will ride roughshod over the honest farmers and craftsmen. However evil and treacherous their lord was, the people do not deserve to suffer now that he is gone."

"Good luck," I tell him. He would make a fine ruler. "I hope you will bring peace to them as well...but remember that blood spilled will only call out for more blood." A fact I know only too well.

"I will do my best to govern wisely and well. But my father will be lord here for some time yet to come. I have time to seek my own destiny, to further my own boundaries. The future will be prosperous for us all." He shakes off his reminiscing. "My father sends thou both his hopes for a safe journey, even if he cannot be present in person to wish thee farewell."

"I spoke with him earlier and heard him speak those same words. I will return to see thou both."

A guard approaches and whispers into his ear. Bastian frowns and sends the man away with a quickly muttered order.

"What is it?" I ask.

"Some of the bodies of the Norsemen have gone missing," he tells us with a small frown twisting his mouth. "Bodies have been taken from the town and Keep. They had all been dumped into the great pit to the east and were to be buried there...some have gone missing it seems."

I shrug. "Grave robbers? Peasants seeking vengeance."

"Perhaps the gravediggers simply miscounted in their haste to bury the pagans. It matters little to us now." Bastian waves to us. "Good journey to thou both. May God watch over thee and guide thy steps."

"Long life to thee and thy family," I reply.

Livia adjusts her hood again. The scent of my sun ointments is strong around her. "Long life,"

Livia says to him. "And keep thy god's feeble blessing to thyself." She flicks her reins and her horse settles into a gentle canter.

I follow and Livia and I ride into the west.

Chapter Eight

The week Livia and I spent on the road passed us by in surprising swiftness. We sought to cover as much ground as possible, riding from late afternoon through the dawning of each new day.

Indeed, it was only due to Livia's continuing insistence and the obvious exhaustion of our horses that we sought shelter beneath the canopy of the forest during the middle of each day. Even after all the time recently spent outside with me and walking upon the battlements of Keep Harfleur, she still refused to fully trust in my herbal potions to protect her pale skin from the sun. I teased her by riding with my hood thrown back and my cloak open as if I sought to regain the bronzed skin of my now centuries-distant youth.

"Thou might trust the moldy potions of thy herbalist friends, but my skin be more sensitive,"

she tells me one afternoon as we rest beneath a canopy of pine branches. "You and I do be creatures of the night, Franc. Our Kind are beings of shadow and soft whispers in the twilight. As it should be."

She smiles. "Our powers weaken in the harsh light of day."

I nod. "I will accept thy point." In the depths of night I can have the strength to slay a hundred men if I so choose. Or I can jump down from some ledge or perch to the ground a score or more paces below and land without feeling any strain in my muscles and joints. Such was not the case during the last battle at Keep Harfleur.

"Even with these potions and herbs, we become little more than mortals. Our skin does not wither nor char, yet we lack our strength and agility and our...." She falls silent.

"Our what?" I prompt.

"Look at the plumage on that jay!" she calls out. "'Tis beautiful."

I can only shake my head at her less-than-subtle change of subject. "Indeed, 'tis a true beauty."

I take a sip of water from my canteen. It slackens my obvious thirst, though it is but the palest shadow of what a true feeding is. The most intoxicating wine cannot come close.

That night, it rains and Livia takes obvious pleasure galloping her mare through the driving rain and fog. Her cloak becomes sodden and heavy, as does my own, and yet she rides with her hood thrown back and her moist lips bared as if she feeds herself upon the storm's fury. Tonight she truly seems to be one of the Fey Folk, a goddess of the hunt given the flesh of a radiant woman.

We ride along the ocean, cantering through the shallows while bypassing a large curve in the road and saving nearly a league on our journey.

We ride through lush forest, seeing naught but a handful rabbits and squirrels.

We ride past farms and manor houses. We see peasants working their fields, craftsmen laboring in their shops, and noblemen surveying their holdings. None both to accost us as we ride by with narry a look or thought to them.

"Mortals are like cattle...a herd to be tended only when necessary."

"And culled as well?"

Mounted carefully on Nightbreeze's back, Livia nods. "When necessary."

I can hear neither sadness nor regret in her tone. She truly looks upon humans in that fashion. I shake my head. Such is a failing with my Kind. Too many of them fail to recall their origins as humble mortals. They have the powers of gods and view themselves accordingly. Such is not always the case....

And so the days passed until we finally crest a small rise and slow our horses to a stop. Both of us take a moment to stare at the port-town spread out along the edge of the sea.

Near mid-afternoon, Livia and I enter the town mounted on our steeds. We pass through an open gate in the wooden wall, nodding politely to the men-at-arms standing guard there. Aside from a searching glance, they take no overt notice of either of us. 'Tis no more than they give to the people on foot passing them by, or the wagons rolling past. The dirt-packed road becomes muddy street and the crowds grow thick. Despite the recent storms, the road has remained passable, the dirt packed solid by the passage of seemingly endless traffic. I have to wonder for a moment why the town's streets have turned into ankle-deep mud.

The main streets are wide, though I tend to avoid them and travel along the alleys and lesser ways, making better time than attempting to fight through the crowds.

I glance back over my shoulder to check that Livia is following close behind. In the thickening crowds, she could easily become separated from me.

If she becomes lost, I will not waste any time looking for her...and she knows this fact without my having to explain it. She would do the same if she was leading us.

A dog comes out of an alley and barks loudly at us before turning and scampering away.

"I hate dogs. So ill-mannered compared to a well-bred cat." Livia sighs briefly. "How much farther?" she demands of me.

"Soon, methinks. This way was once a short-cut." As my steed passes a laden wagon, I sigh aloud for the street ahead is clogged with wains and carts. Even the foot traffic slows down to a near crawl. "I do not recall this town being quite so crowded the last time I passed through it."

"And when was that?" Livia asks as several children run past her.

I have to search my memory for the date of that visit. I had been fleeing from a bad experience with a Centurion named Vettius in Rome. "About three centuries ago," I reply at last. Give or take a decade or two that is.

Livia sighs.

"I think Le Havre had about twenty huts still occupied at the time. A bathhouse. Possibly a small fort, but I cannot honestly recall. Most of the place was in ruins. The port was used only by local fishermen." It has grown up considerably since then.

The entire city seems crowded with peasants and farmers. And the market square which is near to our destination is quite simply packed. People haggle loudly—as if the louder each person can shout will lead to a cheaper bargain—and peddlers call out the names of their wares. Cages stacked up near parked wagons hold scores of chickens, whose clucking fills the air. Sheep tethered near the northern edge of the market baa. I do not see any cows, yet I am certain that there must be some nearby as well.

Surely half the city be gathered here.

I ride calmly through the bedlam with scarcely a look at the market or its countless denizens.

Weavers and tanners and pottery makers all display their wares on tables or upon brightly-coloured cloths spread on the ground. Food-sellers offer fresh fruit or roasted meats. One covered wagon looks to be a tavern on wheels, its back laden with kegs and barrels. It is doing a brisk business.

Livia does look around. Occasionally she reins in her mare for a moment to gaze at some item being displayed. And she invariably dismisses the vendor with a haughty sniff and knees Nightbreeze into slowly following after me.

I laugh.

A man approaches and offers a skewer of meat to me. "A few silvers, sir," he calls out, "and thou will dine well this day." Smoke is still rising from the skewer.

"Be that rabbit?" I ask him. "Or beef?"

"It be rat more likely," Livia mutters. "Look at how he's charred the morsel. 'Tis ruined."

The man glares at Livia. "I would serve no rat!"

"Be gone," she snaps at him. "We are not hungry for thy charcoal." As he scurries back into the crowd and disappears from our sight, she chuckles. "Not hungry for such as he offers that is."

I glance at her. "Try not to drool overmuch, my Lady."

Her snort is not very ladylike.

The harbour is fairly busy. Nearly half a dozen large ships are anchored at the wooden docks.

Sailors and labourers work to load and unload cargo. Out in the sea, I can see nearly a score of smaller boats plying the waves. Fishermen methinks, for the boats seem too small to be sea-worthy. But then I am no sailor. Mayhap they are coastal skimmers.

"Mayhap we can find a ship docked here to bear us north to the Norselands," I tell Livia.

"Then thou are set upon this plan?" she asks me. Her hood is still drawn up, carefully, to shield her pale skin from the sunlight reflecting from the waves.

"Aye." The Norselands beckon clearly to me.

"So be it." She sighs once again. She certainly seems put upon by this entire journey and yet my every suggestion that she might go elsewhere is met with disdain and summarily dismissed.

"Mayhap we should seek a tavern. No doubt the sailors of these boats frequent such places."

"Thou do not need accompany me," I remind her once again. "My journey be not thine. I do not require thee to travel thither with me."

"Yet my steps do follow thine...for good or ill, I feel that I am fated to accompany thee on this journey." She laughs then, an amused giggle that draws looks from more than a few of the passing peasants and dock laborers. "And we cannot argue with fate." She licks her lips as she stares at one tall blond lad as he walks past carrying a large barrel in his arms. "Nor can we long resist the pangs of hunger."

"Indulge thy appetite then," I tell her, "'for the voyage will be long and we will not be able to feed until we set foot upon the Norseland shores." However long that journey will take....

"Another hardship." She shakes her head. "I hope that this talisman be worth all of this effort that thou seem to think it be."

Chapter Nine

The ship looks to be good, large in size, with tall masts for sails, and the look of a stable sea-faring vessel. Or at least as far as I can tell being a man who has spent the vast majority of his life on dry land.

Livia simply shrugs when I ask her opinion of the ship before us. "A boat is a boat," she tells me in a rather absentminded voice. "Choose what thou will."

The wooden sides seem stout and I can see neither moss or rot marring the hull. I cannot smell any decay either—but then the strong salt-scent of the sea breeze mingles with tar and fish to mask any smells but they even to my nose.

Livia's nose is wrinkling more than a rabbit's.

"Not the most congenial garden scents, eh my lady?"

"'Tis bearable," she replies in a bored tone. She stills the twitching of her Romanesque nose. "I have smelled far worse in my time, Franc." She does flick the edge of her cloak forward to further cover her hands. And then she seems to drift away, her thoughts carrying her from the town and away from me. I offer one or two other comments but she ignores them, not even deigning to acknowledge my presence at her side.

What can she be thinking?

The ship's captain is easy to spot, given his stance atop a barrel and the loudness of his voice as he bellows out orders to the roughly-dressed men loading crates onto one of the docked ships.

"Excuse us, good sir, but might thou be the captain of this fine vessel?" I can certainly hazard a guess that it is a fine vessel. Surely he would not be loading a ship that was not seaworthy, for what man would sail upon a ship he knew would surely sink? Then again, what do I know of sailors either?

For all that I know next to nothing about ships save that I have little desire to actually travel upon one, I carry the equal knowledge that only by taking ship can we hope to reach the Norselands in any reasonable amount of time.

The man slowly turns to stare at us with big dark brown eyes. "Aye, I be Nikolas Sorenson.

Kepten and owner of the Starlight Mist." His reddish hair falls to his shoulders, the color matching his beard. his tunic and cloak are cut a well-woven dark cloth so that he seems prosperous.

"I be Franc Nidus and this be my lady friend, Livia Auerillius. We two seek passage to the Norselands...to the realm of the Danes methinks."

"Thou would seek out the halls of Hothgar?" he asks us with a laugh.

"Mayhap that would do for a start."

Nikolas runs a hand through his thick dark beard and then nods to us. "I do sail that way on the morning tide. At least as far as Hedeby, near the halls of Siggardson. He might not be as well-known as Hothgar, yet thou will need not worry that some swamp monster will seek to dine upon thy sleeping body in the night." He chuckles at that. "Passage there be twenty silver crowns apiece." His eyes alight on our horses and his mouth narrows. "I will not carry thy steeds. Twill be too long a voyage for thy animals on my poor ship."

"An acceptable price for the voyage, Kepten. The steeds will not be ours for much longer...they will be of little importance to the rest of the journey we must take." Easy come and thus easy go. I glance at Livia who does not seem to have even noticed the exchange. "Do thou have cabins aboard?"

"Aye. Small and cramped and with few frivolities." He looks long at Livia, obviously appraising her. What little he can see of her beneath her cloak at any rate. "I do not carry many women and those I do carry be used to hardship and cramped quarters. I do not cater to pampered ladies and their whims."

That comment seems to awaken her pride, and she sits up straighter in her saddle and even throws back her cloak, thus exposing her slender form to his gaze. "I will survive this voyage with whatever hardships thou insist upon," she replies in a haughty tone. Her eyes have a chill to them.

He judges us a moment in silence and then nods. "Then return here ere night falls to be settled aboard. We sail on the tide, with or without ye." He glances back at the loading, hastily gauging the progress. At his sudden glare, several crewmen begin to move considerably faster. "Thou eat what the crew eats. The food will be filling if not varied."

"I do not eat much."

"Nor do I." I hand Sorenson several coins in deposit. "And the same again when we return," I promise him.

"Ere nightfall," he reminds us as he pockets the coins.

"We must sell the steeds," I tell Livia as we slowly ride away from the docks.

"Fine. I grow weary of the saddle." She stretches as best she can while still sitting astride her horse. "My bones ache from all this riding. And my bottom might never recover."

"Thy bottom still be a work of art."

She smiles at me, her mood as mercurial as ever. "Ah, the market. Mayhap I will tarry near the weaver. The cloth I saw earlier when we rode past was of a fine weave."

Typical...just about to set off on a grand adventure and she wants to go shopping. "Tomorrow we take ship...the voyage will be different for us both methinks." An errant gust of wind brings a swirl of odors to my nose. Sweat and sewage. Rotting fruit and burned meat. The vaguest hint of musty laundry.

"Aye, but I would not enjoy the hundreds of leagues we must ride by horseback to reach the Danelands." She absently pats Nightbreeze's muzzle. "Thou be a fine mare, but I prefer to journey by carriage."

As I look at the market again a particularly gaunt man catches my eye for an instant before he vanishes back into the crowds gathering around a weaver. He had seemed familiar, tall save for the stooped back of a man aged by harsh labours, white-haired with age....

"I have not been on a ship in nearly twenty years."

Shaking off a sudden chill—no doubt the sudden gust of wind that tugs at my cloak even as it assails my nostrils with the stench of a rotting midden heap—I look at Livia. "Truly?"

"Aye. Not since I crossed the straits from Britannia. I was returning to Rome after a century-long absence. Well," she amends, "mayhap half a century. The incessant rain in Londinium was most wearisome. The sea was rough those two days and I was among the more fortunate of the passengers as I was not violently ill."

"'Tis been many winters since I last took ship," I agree. "And my memories of the voyage are not fond ones." Rough seas and storms had made me miserable, though a band of would-be pirates had livened up the voyage somewhat. A pity that my shipmates had abandoned me on the pirate ship after I revealed my predatory nature and began to slaughter and feed. A lapse of judgement I fear, though understandable given my hunger and the misery with which I endured the rough seas.

Livia prompts her horse into closer pace with mine. "What happened?"

"A violent storm and a shipwreck near Corsica." Mayhap I should not have slain all the pirates while at sea, but who would have thought that a ship would be such a difficult conveyance to master!

So many ropes and sails and what have ye! No wonder that I prefer to travel by horse; tug the reins and it travels as thou command. "It took some luck to survive." Hopefully the experience will not be repeated. "I trust that this journey will fare better. I do not think it be the season of storms yet."

"Nor me. To whom do we sell these beasts?" Livia asks.

"Ever the practical one?" I look at her, taking a moment to gather my thoughts back from the past. "An inn, methinks, might be a wise place to start. Beyond that, mayhap the innkeeper might tell us where we should journey." If all else fails, we can simply leave the horses in a street somewhere.

Sooner or later, someone will lay claim to them and put them to use. I would prefer to sell them though, that we might earn some honest coins which may yet prove useful in the future.

"I will attend to other errands as well."

I follow Livia's line-of-sight to a pair of brawny farmhands. They are both tanned and well-muscled from their livelihoods and attractive of face. Definitely Livia's preferred type for snacking.

"Try not to leave them resting where anyone might stumble across them," I request.

She nods rather resignedly to me. "Do not fear for me, Franc. I have been feeding since before thou crossed the veil to become one of us. Since before your mother's mother was born methinks."

I smile at her. "I have always been fond of older women."

The look she casts me would splinter wood.

Chapter Ten

The ship lurches on the windswept waves.

Standing near the bow, all I can see is grey-blue water as I gaze from horizon to horizon. The moonlight is as bright as day, dazzling and sparkling as if the sea is dusted with jewels. But there is just so much water... Waves stretch off into eternity...how easy to believe in the sailors' tales of sailing a ship right off the edge of the world and into the abyss.

Starlight Mist. 'Tis an ethereal name for a ship which in truth seems to wallow more than glide gracefully across the waves. Who knew that a ship could roll so much? It seems that we spend more time travelling sideways than forwards, twisting back and forth like a lost serpent.

I can hear footsteps on the deck behind me. The soft tread, almost a glide, is most assuredly that of Livia and I can scent her essence lightly upon the breeze. I do not bother to turn away from peering at the endless waves, nor do I remove my hands from the rail. I wish to contemplate the ocean from out here.

"So why is this damned talisman so important to thee?"

Startled by the question, I turn my head to look at Livia. "What do thou mean?"

Clad in a dark blue gown, without her cloak, ghostly in the moonlight, she seems to be a creature of the waves given a solid form and sent to walk amongst men. "Thou only half believe in its existence," she replies with a frown, "and yet thou jump aboard the nearest ship and set sail across the sea to the Norselands in search of it?" She shakes her head now, letting her loose hair fall across her shoulders. "What game do thou think to play at with me?" Her eyes narrow.

"I have all of eternity," I reply with a rather flippant grin. "Perhaps I am undertaking this quest to simply kill some time."

She snorts loudly.

"Perhaps it really does exist…think of what could be done with it." I look at her, narrowing my own eyes as I do so. "What are thy reasons for accompanying me?" I demand of her in turn. "Surely thou do not believe in the legend either."

"Mayhap I do." She shrugs as clouds obscure the moon and cast us both into shadow. Even now both of us can see as plainly as if we stood under a noon sun. "As thou say, if it do exist, then simply think of what might be done with it." Naked hunger and ambition light up her slender face, giving a warm glow to her pale skin. "The power to restore life to the dead, Franc!"

"A true prize for such as we. A means to take us back beyond the Veil to our mortal lives."

"To grow old and withered and weak and then finally to die? I will pass on such a prize," Livia tells me, "but with the talisman one could live forever!"

"Eternal life without needing to feed?" That would appeal to many of my Kind.

"'Tis a gift that every mortal hungers for."

"And most of our Kind too, I dare think."

"No doubt." She shrugs, dismissing our brethren from her thoughts. "With possession of a magical talisman capable of such a feat, I could become unto a goddess!" Livia's laughter blends with the wind into a cruel sound that seems to disturb even the sky as the handful of clouds break up and scatter.

* * *

The moon is once again high and bright in the sky, reflecting off the water as we sail northward.

I have ventured onto the deck to look around, unable to rest in my small cabin. I have never traveled by ship for such a long time before—over a quarter-moon has passed since I have last set foot on dry land—and the endless waves disturb me with their soft splashing against the hull of the boat. I fear that I grow restless.

Livia worries me. What might she get up to out here? She is used to diversions and merriment and crowds. This quiet near solitude at sea might prove more than she can readily handle. Will she seek to ply her tricks upon some member of the crew?

My mood is not helped any by that sense that I have of being watched. 'Tis the same feeling I had while being spied upon by some unseen watcher in Myrddin's forest, but I know that we are currently many leagues away from the shore and far beyond the gaze of anyone. Even the crew of the Starlight Mist slumber peacefully in their bunks, save for one or two men who bear the necessary duty of the night watch.

A shadow moves on the far side of the deck, gliding gracefully across the planks with scarcely a sound. I stand by the main mast, still as a carved statue, watching the other figure. Then I allow the wind that fills the sails to tug at the edge of my cloak and the soft flapping sound causes the other to give a little start

I look at Livia as she finally approaches me. "Thou seem satisfied this night." Why she is, I cannot place, but her sudden contentedness worries me. 'Tis not like her.

"I am, Franc." She seems to be at her ease, content like a recently-fed cat lounging in the sunlight, save that it is by moonlight that I now gaze upon her.

"What have thou done?" I demand harshly.

"What might I have done?" she counters with a soft laugh. She waves one beringed hand to gesture at the waves. "There be not much to do on this oversized raft." She giggles and grips at the rail for balance as the boat crests a particularly large wave.

I shake my head in resignation. I will not even try to play games with her when she is in this mood. 'Tis not worth the effort. "Good night then." I retire to my cabin and blow out my candle.

But even while laying in my bunk and wrapped in my blankets, I am unable to sleep. When I close my eyes, I see Livia's contented smile on her face.

I feel a sense of doom hanging coldly in the air.

The morning comes and I awake to shouts and calls and the sudden thumps of the crew moving about and searching for something. Or someone.

After hastily anointing my face and hands with some of my sun lotions and donning my cloak, I venture from my cabin and onto the deck. I step through the hatch and then can only stand and blink in the dazzling sunlight. If the moon made the waves sparkle, then the sun duplicates the effect a thousandfold. "What be the cause of such bother, Kepten?" I ask. I pull the hood of my cloak forward to shield my eyes from the glare.

Sorenson looks at me with a frown set upon his face. "I do be missing one of me crew," he replies grimly. "Tyrson vanished in the night." He runs a hand through his beard.

I look around—the sea stretches away to all horizons. "Out here?"

"Aye. At first I thought that he had taken some ale from the galley and fallen asleep where none might stumble across him. But we have checked everywhere and he cannot now be found." He turns back to staring at the sea. "Helvete," he swears softly.

I look at him and then turn my gaze towards the waves that trail behind us. There is absolutely nowhere for a missing man to go...save overboard.

My blue eyes narrow as a dark thought takes form.

"Of course I dined last night." Livia does not sound the least bit apologetic as I question her sharply in my cramped cabin. She does keep her voice down, for neither of us wish to have our conversation be overheard by Sorenson or any of his crew. "Unlike thee, I did not gorge myself upon Norsemen at Keep Harfleur. I have certain appetites, Franc, and I cannot contain my nature forever."

She smiles smugly. "It has been nearly a quarter-moon since I dined last, back in port." She turns away from me and takes a step across what little open floor my cabin contains. "And those young farm boys were pleasant enough to look at, if not overly filling."

I stare at her back for a moment and then I grip her arm and twirl her around to face me. My angry expression has been known to send even mighty warriors seeking cover and yet she fails to even flinch.

In truth, her smile never wavers.

"We be on a ship!" I remind her in a sharp voice. "Thy careless actions have raised a hue and cry from the Starlight's crew!"

"So what?" She shakes her head disdainfully. "The mortals have no cause for complaint nor alarm. None saw me dine, nor were any awake to see a lone man fall silent and helpless into the sea."

"How could thou be so foolish?"

"I was hungry."

I slap the smile from her face. "Do not feed again until we reach land," I order her in a stern tone. "Else thou will face my wrath."

For a moment the glare on her face seems cold enough to freeze even the horizonless ocean solid, but then abruptly she smiles at me. "As thou wish, Franc," she replies in a soft tone. She has her head bowed so that I cannot see her eyes.

Chapter Eleven

"There stands the port of Hedeby."

It is a sprawling seaport town. Around the water-filled bowl of the harbour, the streets of houses and shops seem to stretch inland for miles. A trick of the eyes, but a daunting view nonetheless.

Low hills rise up, lifting the houses and shops of the town above the harbour and thus, further the illusion of the town's sheer size.

Stone quays thrust into the water like the grasping fingers of some monstrous and ravenous beast, and scores of boats—ranging from small fishing craft to ships which dwarf the Starlight Mist—are tied to them. What looks like hundreds of men labour to load and unload cargo from the myriad ships.

"There must be thousands there," Livia whispers in what I must call a reverent tone of voice.

Her eyes bounce across the shore, feasting upon the looks of man after man.

"'Tis a major trading centre for these parts," Sorenson reminds us. "Indeed, a centre for all of Europe methinks. Some say there do be fifteen thousand souls living within the city. It thrives upon trade and upon the work of those who travel the seas."

So many people...so many potential meals. "Impressive, Kepten. A most impressive claim." I pause a moment to force all thoughts of feeding from my mind. I will not indulge my carnal tastes recklessly, or so I tell myself. I am on a quest after all and I must remain focussed upon the completion of said quest. "'Tis a rival for Imperial Rome herself," I muse aloud. "Or fair Paris."

"Both of those do be fine cities," Sorenson agrees, "and I have seen them both and wandered amongst their streets and bargained in their shops. But Hedeby is far more than a mere port. This be the heart of the Norselands. Aye, the very beating heart."

"Then it be a worthy place to start our search." I gaze at the rows of streets leading away from the crowded docks. "Surely there be someone here who might tell us of what we wish to learn." The real question, of course, would be how to find him, or her.

"A library mayhap?" one of the sailors working nearby asks.

"Aye, that would do nicely. Ragmussen be thy name?" I think that is how he was named to us earlier. Despite our many days on the ship, the sailors all look very much the same to me and their names remain mostly a mystery.

"Aye, that be my name. Olaf Ragmussen." He straightens from his task of coiling up a long rope and walks towards us. "Some of the local lords might be pleased if thou should call upon them. I do know one, for he do be a distant cousin of mine." He rubs his hands on his brown tunic.

Sorenson nods at that and gestures with his hand towards the city. "Guvenor Siggardson's hall be built up on that hill." He points to one particular hill and the wooden hall built atop it. "Mayhap I can find thou a suitable guide to take thou there."

"That will not be necessary...the hall should be easy enough to find." We need only follow a road leading in that direction after all. Standing atop that hill, it should be readily visible to us at all times. "Should we become lost I have no fear to asking for directions from a shopkeeper or some passerby." Although I am not certain if the city's governor would wish to see us so readily when we do arrive at his gates.

"Nay, 'tis much effort for ye. If I recall correctly Ragmussen doth have business there this very day."

The other man nods his balding head. "Aye, Kepten. I do need to speak with my kinsman about spices and other such cargo that he did wish us to gather for him from the east."

Sorenson smiles widely as if that simple fact decides matters. "Excellent, eh Franc? Olaf will guide thee there and introduce thee and thy lady to the lord's retainers." He smiles behind his thick beard.

"Enjoy the weather and dress well...this be the warm part of the day." He turns and strides across the deck. "Ready the oars!" he shouts to his crew. "Ready to cast ropes to shore!"

"Warm?" Livia grumbles as she joins us at last. "This be colder than the frigidarium in the baths in Rome." She draws her cloak more tightly around her shapely form. "I thought that I would freeze ere he finished talking of his cousin and the city."

"The cold does not bother me," I reply. "We are beyond such petty concerns," I add in a softer tone.

"Thou might be, yet I still feel the cold burning my bones." She shivers and casts a glance over her shoulder at the hatch leading back to her cabin.

I laugh aloud.

The streets of Hedeby are just as crowded with people as we had expected. There are some wagons and carts being pulled by mules and horses, but mostly the traffic is composed merely of common people on foot. The streets are hard-packed dirt, though I suspect the lesser lanes and alleys are more likely to be the sticky mud which plagues all towns. Cobblestone roadways are a rare sight.

The town has many trees growing along the streets, between houses and by the roadside which make it seem less civilized than the great cities of my youth. I take note of numerous trees with fallen branches, as if lightning had struck them repeatedly.

"Nay," says our balding guide when I mention my thoughts to him. "Odin did not practice any of his spear throwing here. The trees do simply burst from the cold."

"From the cold?" Livia repeats with a frown upon her face.

"Aye...course, there do be more bursting this winter than 'tis strictly normal."

Livia and I exchange looks of surprise. Trees bursting from the cold? I can only shake my head at the thoughts that this what happens during in a normal winter! What a desolate and harsh land this is.

"Surely thou jest!" Livia protests at last.

"Nay, my Lady. 'Tis a common enough sight hereabouts." Ragmussen draws his cloak closer about himself as a chill wind slices at us. "But this past winter did be more harsh than 'tis usual for our land." His eyes rest for a moment on a cold-shattered tree. "But I admit that these breaks leave me puzzled."

"And why is that?" I ask.

"Why 'tis only October."

Livia smiles warmly at a tall merchant's guard who is staring appreciatively at her. "I know the month it doth be." He looks to be her preferred type.

"Aye, my Lady." Ragmussen wipes the top of his bare scalp with his hand. "But 'tis too early for such a cold to strike us. Too early by far...."

I toss a small coin to a peddler standing at the mouth of an alley and take a skewer of meat from his fire. "This be rabbit?" I ask him.

He nods. "Aye, good master."

I take a careful bite. "Not bad." It was poorly cooked, the outside charred and the inside still pink. Almost raw. And quite delicious. I buy another.

* * *

The governor's hall looks to be stoutly made. Tall wooden walls rise some three stories at their peak. Numerous windows, all tightly shuttered against the coming night. A door of thick oak stands open, with an equally thick bar waiting to fall into place once it is closed. Three men in fur-lined cloaks stand near the door, warming their hands over a small fire crackling there, and softly talking amongst themselves.

"They prepare for the night." Ragmussen begins to walk faster along the road. "We will not wish to be caught out of doors this night. Another storm is coming."

I can see the clouds rolling in from the north. They stretch across the blue sky like a dark shroud. The wind is picking up again, chill enough to make our breath visible in the air.

"Once we have found the talisman, I shall retire to the warm southlands," Livia grumbles.

"Mayhap the sands of Egypt will welcome me once again."

I shake my head. "Thou can keep the sands, for I found that land to dry for my taste." I do not care for the priests and their rituals either. "I will remain in the forests here. Or mayhap I shall travel into the east once more." I no longer know if I am doing the right thing by coming here...following hunches and voices whispering quietly in my dreams. I, who have not dreamed since before crossing over the Veil.

"Hej!" Ragmussen calls to the guards.

They look at him and raise their hands in greeting.

I am happy that they seem to recognize our guide, and happier still that they leave their swords sheathed. I am not in the mood for a fight.

"I have come as promised," Ragmussen tells them. "I seek leave to stop beneath this roof."

"Thou have our leave to pass through the gates, Olaf," the oldest of the guards replies. "Lord Siggardson will decide if thou are worthy of guest-right."

"Tak, Kepten. Thou need not summon a servant, for I know the way." He looks back at us as the captain nods. "I spent the better times of my childhood in this hall."

* * *

"'Tis just through here." Ragmussen pushes open a door and steps into a small hall. He has led us quickly through numerous torch-lit corridors, around a dozen corners, and finally stops at one particular door. And he had only paused once to ask a serving wench where Siggardson currently could be found.

"Thy memory be good."

"I did grow up amongst these very walls. One does not forget the tracks where one wandered as a child."

I nod agreement with his words. I can recall the forest trails and narrow caves where I had played in my youth with such detail that I can still smell the decaying leaves.

The room beyond the door is lit by a fire crackling in a large firepit and by torches along the wall. Tapestries cover the rough wooden planks with brightly woven pictures. An old man stands near the firepit, leaning on a thick stick while warming his hands, and a dozen or so other men of lesser age are gathered near him. They are all silent, listening to a young man in a blue tunic declaim in a clear voice as he plucks at a harp.

"I died as a mammal and became a plant.

I died as a plant and became an animal.

I died as an animal and I was a man.

Why should I fear?

When was I ever less by dying?

Yet, once more I shall die,

to soar in the Blessed Realm;

but even from Godhood I must pass on."

"A good recitation of The Mathnawi," one of the men says. "Thy studies proceed apace."

"He learns well," the old man agrees, "but there be many tales and lessons yet for him to master before he might be considered a proper harper."

The young man bows his head humbly and whispers "Tak".

The first speaker nods. "He shall learn, Guvenor."

Ragmussen gestures to the old man standing near the firepit. "Hail, cousin!" he calls out. "This be Lord Siggardson, the governor of the city," he adds in a softer tone for our benefit.

"Olaf! I had hoped to see thee again. I knew not that the Mist had docked this day." With a broad smile on his face, Siggardson leaves his fellows and approaches us quickly to embrace his cousin in a strong hug. "Welcome home. And who be thy companions?"

"I be Franc Nidus of Gaul, and my companion be Lady Livia Auerillius, late of Rome."

She curtsies to him, keeping her eyes downcast in a demure fashion. She plays the role of the perfect lady quite nicely. "I am honoured to meet thee, my Lord."

The old man takes her hand carefully and raises it to hips lips and kisses it. "Nay, 'tis we who be honoured by thy presence here, my Lady. Thy beauty is surely a gift to thee by the goddesses."

She smiles, the warm expression casting a radiant glow to her pale face. "Thank ye, my Lord."

She does enjoy receiving compliments.

"A fine lady and thou, my cousin. In the same night as Haakon himself rests beneath my roof."

He smiles even more widely. "The Aesir look most kindly upon me this night." He raises his voice.

"Ale and mead for my guests!" he calls out to his servants. "Thou must dine with me."

Ragmussen nods eagerly. "I look forward to feasting at thy table. 'Tis been too long at sea.

The delicacies of thy table have been sorely missed whilst we tarried in Normandy."

"We do not wish to be a bother, Guvenor," I choose to protest carefully. "Our path lead us from Normandy to the Norselands. We merely took ship across the sea with thy cousin. When we sought to part ways and seek out an inn, he insisted upon leading us to thy hall."

"As well he should." Siggardson nods happily. "For he knows that I enjoy the company of men from afar. A few tales of place that thou have seen will be welcome by our fires. And thy Lady be a fine guest for any night." He hands her a flagon of mead taken from a newly-arrived servant. "Thou are welcome beneath my roof for as long as thou wish to stay in Hedeby."

"Tak," I reply with a bow.

Chapter Twelve

Keeping my footsteps as light as a autumn-colored leaf falling to the ground, I approach the room where Haakon is spending the night.

I have been lucky, indeed blessed by the gods, that he is right now present within Siggardson's Hall, for his fame as seer is widely known throughout the Norselands and beyond. The servants have spoken of his presence repeatedly and I chanced to overhear their words as I passed them by. He is not given into doing much foretelling these days nor has he stirred from his chambers since arriving in Hedeby some five suns before. Siggardson has spoken well of him, and of his talents, during dinner as well. And so, by moonlight, I creep along the wooden-tiled rooftop to his bedchamber and peer through the half-open shutter.

The room is small and Spartan, with but a single rough pallet placed before the small hearth. At least he has several blankets to keep him warm, I note. A brace of beeswax candles burns on a small table and a fire crackles merrily in the hearth.

Haakon himself is old, with white hair falling down past his shoulders, and a chest-length beard to match. He is clad in a dark green robe and he coughs a bit as he hobbles away from the pallet. It would appear that he has only just risen from a nap.

A small chest is the only other furnishing in the room, the only thing that I can see from my current vantage point at any rate. A small bronze pitcher rests atop it. Might it contain ale or mead, I wonder.

The old man abruptly stops in mid-step on a small rug which is the only floor covering there.

He stands in the centre of the chamber, with his hands held just in front of his solar plexus. "I am within the Light." He twirls his hands. "I am the Light," he places both of his hands on his head, "and the Light goes through me. The Light protects me." He keeps his left hand on his head and thrusts his right hand away from himself. "The Light surrounds me." He crosses his hands in front of, and then behind, his body. "The Light is me." He returns his hands to their original position in front of his solar plexus.

I make no movement, instead watching him intently. A spell of some kind? I do not see anything happening, no obvious signs of magic at work but surely he is doing something mystical. His presence seems muted to my senses, though I suspect that it is because he is so old.

"What do thou seek of me, Man of Gaul?" he asks, suddenly turning to look directly at the window where I stand watching.

How does he know that I am present? He cannot have seen me, surely not through the closed shutters and in the dark night. I made no sound either, no sound loud enough for an elderly mortal to hear that is; even one of my brethren would have been hard-pressed to hear my footsteps above the normal creaking of the Hall. So how did he know? Even as I ponder the mystery, I push the shutters open and swing through them to enter the bedchamber. I offer him a polite nod of greeting and then take a step towards him.

He does not flinch at either my appearance or my abrupt entry. I have left both my cloak and my sword back in my own bedchambers, appearing clad only in a blue tunic and brown breeches. I do not wish to alarm him, so I seek to appear as unthreatening as possible.

My efforts succeed for he does not look frightened of me in the slightest. "Welcome, sir." His voice is comforting, warming like the sweet-scented fire. Apple wood, methinks. "What brings thou to lurk outside of my bedchamber?"

"I am told that thou can foretell the future."

"Aye, such is a gift to me from the Allfather."

"Good Master Haakon, would thou cast my future?" I ask of him. "I face a difficult journey and must know whether my steps be true."

The old seer is silent for a long moment. His eyelids are half-closed, almost as if he is asleep, standing up, and he sways back and forth on his booted feet as if pushed by a slight breeze which only he can feel.

I say nothing more to him. This must be his choice. Instead I further study the room. My first appraisal was correct—the room is Spartan. Even the wooden walls lack decoration, the tapestries and hangings which brighten the rest of the Hall are missing from this chamber.

At last, Haakon nods. "Aye, I shall do this reading for thee, Frank Nidus. I have seen thy face in my dreams, Man of Gaul, and I will cast the Runes for thee."

Does he know my name from overheard gossip or through his arts? His smile is enigmatic, interpretable in many ways. I would dare think that he has heard of my presence through talks with either Siggardson or some of the servants, yet he called me by name ere he could possibly have known that I lurked beyond his window.

"Thy aura is strong and I sense that thou are a true seeker."

"I do what I can."

"Thou seek something, but whether the light or the shadow guides thee I cannot say." Haakon holds up a small deer-skin pouch which he has just untied from his belt. The pouch rattles softly.

"These are the Runes." He sinks down to his knees in a smooth movement. A surprisingly smooth movement for a man of his years, I note. Then he shakes the bag and then pours them onto the floor.

I stare at the small disks of wood. From the rattle, I had expected to see either wood or bone.

These disks be cut from white beech, methinks, roughly rounded, and each bearing a small symbol.

Haakon arranges the runes in a rough circle, face down, without any clue as to which symbol might be hidden. "Name me a number, Franc, greater than ten and less than thirty."

"Twenty-seven," I blurt. It is the first number to pop into my mind. As is the way with many of these rituals, one must trust one's own instincts and speak without forethought...if I try to consciously direct the Casting, then its results will be rendered invalid.

"Place thy finger upon a rune."

I kneel down in front of Haakon and obey his command. All of the disks look alike to me. I close my eyes and, after waving my hand around however the mood takes me for a few moments, let my finger drop until it touches one.

"Thou have chosen Ur," Haakon tells me as he turns it over and stares at a symbol which to my eyes looks like a squared archway. "'Tis the rune of strength." Starting with his finger on the rune directly to right of the one I have chosen, he counts twenty-seven disks which he slowly turns face up.

"Odal." His tone sounds grim.

"Odal?" I repeat. My tone is one of confusion. The rune is a triangle with two legs.

"Separation." The old man pauses a moment in careful thought. "Thou have been separated and thou seek to find that which thou have lost." He stares down at the runes and then turns one of them face up, seemingly chosen at random. "Thorn, a gateway to someplace. Eh which is movement...thou are on a journey to somewhere..." He turns up a third disk. "Daeg...a breakthrough of sorts. Hmm..."

The first three symbols chosen so rapidly look like a squared off 'P', an 'M', and an hourglass laying on its side. I look at the fourth rune. It is blank. Blank on both sides.

"Wyrd, the unknowable." Haakon stares at me with his piercing blue eyes. "Thy journey's end is cloaked from my eyes. I cannot tell thee which path to walk." He lowers his head, until his bearded chin rests upon his chest, almost sadly.

"A pity then."

His head lifts. "But I can tell thou this and take what comfort thou can from my words. Thy path does lead into the mountains...to the Frost Giant's teeth." He scoops the Runes up from the floor and stuffs them back into his pouch. "Now go. Leave me to my night's rest." He coughs again as I stand up and walk towards the door. "And know one thing more, Man of Gaul."

"What?" I ask, my hand resting on the latch of the chamber door.

The candles on the table choose that moment to flicker and go out, plunging the room into darkness. Haakon's voice seems to reach my ears as if from a considerable distance. "There is a darkness is lurking in the shadows...a storm is coming to shake Midgard. The frost giant will be waiting for thee and the wyrm lurks in its heart."

Chapter Thirteen

"But how do I find the teeth of a frost giant?" I muse aloud, while staring down at the scroll in my hand. Livia is seated beside me, studying the old scroll as well.

"They be all around thee." Siggardson tells me calmly as he settles himself into a nearby chair and lifts his flagon of ale to his lips.

I have not even noticed him drawing near to us, despite his leaning upon a stick. The hall is crowded with men gathered in many groups, drinking and boasting. The only women I see around are the wenches serving the men, buxom maidens hefting platters of roasted boar and jugs of ale and of mead.

"Thy lands be plagued with frost giants then?"

"Aye, Lady Livia, some parts of it do still be. These lands hereabouts be at peace though."

Siggardson smiles at her. "There has not been a frost giant threatening Hedeby in some hundred winters."

"Just a hundred winters past, eh?" I ask. "Was it a big one?"

"'Twas not the largest of giants, no," Siggardson admits that fact in an almost mournful tone of voice. "Nor did I see the monster myself. My grandsire did tell me of it though. As tall as a house this one stood."

"Just a small giant then."

"Aye, Franc. 'Tis much too warm this far south for the true giants to roam widely. I am told, however, that in the most northern fiords, frost giants scrape the clouds with their helmets. They pick at their teeth with tall pines and crush boulders into dust for sport. Their bones be the stuff of the very living mountains and their hides be tougher than dragon-scale."

"I have heard similar stories," I admit.

"These be the true words of my grandsire," Siggardson protests. "He did face a frost giant in his youth."

"And he lived to tell the tale of his bold deed?"

"He had success in his quest for the Aesir were on his side."

I hold up my flagon so that a swerving wench can refill it with more the heady ale which is being served so freely. 'Tis almost strong enough to addle my wits. "If I recall the old tales correctly, the only person that the frost giants ever feared was Thor."

"Aye. With his mighty hammer, Thor could slay a frost giant with little effort. 'Twas all but a simple game to him. A means to pass the time."

A shout bellows from the group of men gathered near the firepit as one among them loses an arm wrestling bout. More shouts herald the beginning of a second match.

"So where might we find one?" Livia asks our host. "Haakon told Franc that he must seek out the Frost Giant's heart."

"Nay," I correct her, "he said that I must venture to the frost giant's teeth." I lower my voice.

"He said that a wyrm laired in its heart."

Livia sniffs and draws her cloak more tightly around herself.

"The mountains be the teeth of a frost giant. Everyone knows that." Siggardson pauses while the wind gusts around the walls and whistles through the smoke-hole in the roof. "The Fenris Wolf howls loudly this night," he says in a low tone, casting a nervous glance over his shoulder at the tightly shuttered windows. "Twill not be a good night for venturing beyond the doors." I can smell traces of fear emanating from him.

I note Livia's sudden glance of interest and thus I narrow my eyes. What has caught her attention now? "How often does this wolf howl?"

"Often enough, Franc. Every winter he seeks to break free from his Dwarf-forged chains and devour the sun...some day he will succeed and the entire world will be plunged into darkness and Ragnarok will come." Through some bizarre, and unsettling, coincidence, the rest of the room falls into silence at the mention of Ragnarok. "'Tis the death of humankind," the old man murmurs.

"Gotterdamung. The very fall of the gods themselves." He shrugs and lowers his head as he stares into the crackling fire. "The end of everything."

"A cheerful thought." Livia's tone is one of disgust.

"Aye," I agree with her in a low tone, "but 'tis the way of the Norsemen. The prophecy by which their world was born and thus shall die. A harsh belief for a harsh land."

The noise level of the room returns to its previous levels. Calls of ale and mead echo from a score of thirsty throats.

"I am just worried about what else might be found within these lands...how many others might already be here, seeking that which we seek."

"I suspect that few will come to seek it, Livia." I sip from my flagon. Aye, this ale be heady indeed; strong enough to drug a dragon into slumber! "Who knows of it besides Ulric and ourselves?"

I ask her with a shrug. "And Ulric be dead."

"Ulric, the Witch King?" Siggardson asks in surprise. His brow furrows as his blue eyes stare at the two of us. The flagon of ale in his hand is shaking, spilling ale onto the rush-covered floor.

"Aye."

"Thou have tangled with him?" His voice is quiet, low enough that I must strain to hear his words. He has turned pale.

"Aye, and lived to tell the tale it seems. He be dead now." I can sense fear in the air. Strong fear.

"So say thou...I will not be quick to accept such a tale until I see the body burned and the ashes scattered in the deepest sea." He shivers and huddles deeper into his rich robes. "All hereabouts know of the Witch King."

"We are not from here," Livia reminds him. "Tell us about him then...why should the people hereabouts fear him?"

Siggardson looks at her as if she is mad. "Because he is a potent sorcerer!" he says. "He rose up from a poor farmer's son to become a man to whom even great chieftains bowed and paid vast tributes. Legend speaks of him being a mischievous child in his youth, the very spawn of Loki himself, who constantly sought out the teachings of hedge wizards and witches rather than tend to his father's flocks. He was an adventuresome man in his prime, wandering far from his homelands to explore and learn what he could of the wider world. He was still an ambitious greybeard in my own grandfather's youth, before his rise to full power.

"For 'tis rumoured and told that the Witch King made terrible promises to the frost giants and the dwarves in exchange for learning their ancient knowledge, and thus he gained much power through his dark sorcery. Some say that he himself harbored the blood of a frost giant within his veins." The fear scent is growing stronger. "Over time, he grew powerful enough to dare to challenge the gods, even Odin the Allfather himself."

"I see." 'Tis a pretty enough story. I glance at Livia.

She is listening to our host with rapt attention, her eyes wide and her lips half open.

"He was mad to make such boasts, and madder still to attempt to fulfill them." Siggardson shakes his head grimly. "The Witch King—we do not speak his name even now—kept the Norselands in a state of dread for many winters. His dark hall stood as a blight upon the land, and all knew of it and avoided the spot. Only those who were touched by darkness would venture there, and even then many of them took pains to avoid being summoned thither. For long years he ruled over the land, commanding all others to obey and sending his minions riding forth to collect wealth and sacrifices as he wished.

"But the Witch King failed to reckon with the weakness of his followers. Whilst he led a raid against the Rus, seeking greater tributes and new slaves to be sacrificed in his foul rituals, the tribes nearest to his home rebelled and overthrew the chiefs who had sworn their own souls to him. The Witch King returned to find his allies slaughtered or scattered, and his home burned to the ground."

"And he did something truly horrible?" I ask, sensing how the story would now shift.

"Aye, for we had forgotten that his power lay in death and decay. Slaughtering his followers only seemed to increase his power, and his rage was already a thing of legend." His hand tightens around his stick. "And then we did see his wrath in action.

"He swore a terrible vengeance upon all in the Norselands—summoning forth a curse of pestilence and famine." Siggardson seems to have aged visibly as he relates the tale to us. A mighty leader of a prosperous town reduced to an old man cowering by a fire. "Many perished in that terrible winter. Entire villages and towns were wiped out overnight, the people and their herds and flocks vanishing without a trace or else dying in the most horrible ways. Convulsions. Foaming at the mouth.

Screaming in agony. Their very bones snapping as they writhed in the grips of the curse.

"But the tribes rallied around their greatest warriors and heroes. They marched against the Witch King, even to the gates of his newly rebuilt hall, and his remaining followers were slain in a great battle. The hall was burned to the ground and the very earth itself was salted. The Witch King, however, escaped justice by fleeing to the sea, using his sorcery to summon forth a terrible storm that sank many of the long ships which sought to pursue him. His own dragon boat vanished into the sea, into the very storm he had summoned, and he has not been seen for many winters since...."

Even I feel some chill from that story. I sip from my ale to banish my discomfort as something tickles at my mind. "How many winters ago did all this happen?"

"'Twas some fifty winters ago, if I recall correctly for I was but a small boy, when the Witch King was finally banished. My father did fight in the last battle though, and helped to cleanse the Norselands of the Witch King's foul legacy."

"Fifty winters ago when he was banished?" And him already a greybeard in Siggardson's grandfather's youth? "Surely that is too long...he cannot be that old." Had the sorcerer truly seen over a hundred winters before his disappearance at sea?

"His powers are vast," Siggardson reminds us in a weary voice. "When one is willing to pay any price, then even death might be cheated."

Livia looks at me. "It would seem that we were luckily than I had first thought in our defense of the Harfleurs if such was Ulric's power."

"Speak not his name!"

I glance at Siggardson. "As thou wish." I smile grimly at his superstitious fear.

Chapter Fourteen

"The storm is raging well."

"'Tis winter here, such storms are to be expected." I stare out at the snow for a few moments longer, and then I regretfully pull the shutters closed. I can scarcely see the houses of the town below.

"I do not see us starting our journey this day." It would be madness for us to venture forth...in this unfamiliar country and not clearly knowing whence we journeyed, we would become lost amid the snows for certain.

"That suits me. I enjoy the company here."

I look at her. "Oh?" I ask in a neutral tone of voice.

"Aye." A smile plays at her full lips. "Siggardson be a fine host. He be knowledgeable and mannerly. A change from most of the men I meet."

"Do thou have plans for him?" I ask.

Livia giggles. "Whatever do thou mean?" she counters. "What plans might I have for one such as he?"

"Aye, 'tis a good question. One which bears careful study methinks."

"Franc, be thou jealous?" She sounds surprised. "Thou have rejected me...what should it matter it to thee if I now decide to choose a new mate and guide him across the Veil?"

"No matter to me." I try to keep my tone level.

She giggles again—I know from that sound that I have failed to mask my feelings from her—and then she turns to stare into the crackling fire. "I thought that it would not matter to thee what I do with my life."

I wince at the casualness of her tone. "But remember well what happened the last time thou sought to bring a lover across the Veil."

"That was not my fault," she replies quickly.

"Recall it well nonetheless." It had been a bloody mess. Literally.

"Thou should recall such truths as well," Livia throws back at me. "Thy own attempts at bringing thy past loves across the Veil have not been such grand success stories that thou might be called a master of the art."

I wince again. She is not playing fair this night. "At least my attempt did not burn down half the city when no one would rally to his banner." The lure of godhood could be dangerous enough for mere mortal men, let alone a general who dreamed of becoming emperor.

"'Twas that past and should remain dead to us, yes? Anyway, I have no desire to turn anyone."

She leaves the warmth of the firepit to glide towards me. "I have other matters on my mind, Franc."

Her hair is hanging loosely over her shoulders.

"Such as the Talisman?"

"Aye, there be that. But I did also think of the news I heard from a serving maid this morning."

"What news?"

She smoothes the front of her pale dress with her slender hands. "A man was murdered last night, near the harbor. His throat had been ripped out and yet there was no blood left in his body."

I look at her.

She shakes her head. "It was no doing of mine."

"Nor of mine, Livia." I can only frown at this news. "It seems that we have another of our Kind here."

"And one who be not cautious in how he feeds." Livia snorts. "This be the third man so found within the past quarter-moon. The common folk who are brought across the Veil these days have no respect for tradition, nor do they follow the dictates of common sense. Such behavior will only draw down the pursuit of the mob upon us all." She shivers and rubs her hands along her arms. "I have no desire to be prey to a frenzied mob. I had enough of such excitement during the fall of Rome."

"Which fall?" I ask.

She does not deign to answer.

* * *

I stand on the lonely hilltop as the cold wind gusts around me and tugs fiercely at my fur-lined cloak. I have timed things well, bathing carefully at dusk in a small icy pond, and now midnight approaches even as I finish my preparations. At least it is not snowing, even the sky is mostly clear, save for some clouds shrouding the horizon, and I make my preparations by the light of the moon and stars.

I kindle a fire and let it burn to ashes and embers.

"So bathe in the waters of life," I chant as the scent of the burning incense surrounds me. "To wash off the not-Human, I come in self-annihilation, and the grandeur of inspiration!" I seek answers and the rituals would avail me of some peace of mind. Or so I hope.

My horse neighs from where he has been hobbled. I have borrowed the steed from Siggardson's stables with his blessings. He thinks that I have ridden forth on some idle business of my own, but in truth I have felt myself summoned to do this ritual. And it cannot be conducted properly within the confines and boundaries of either the Hall or the city, so I have journeyed half a day beyond the town before finding the right hilltop. The aura of the place seemed to shine to my eyes, and I knew that this was where I must cast my circle and light the fire.

Even though I almost think that someone has followed me to this place.

I saw no one else on the road, have little fear that anyone could have tracked me without my knowing it. I am a predator by nature and my hunter's instincts be strong. I would swear to the very gods of my people that I am alone here, leagues away from mortal men, and yet the feeling persists.

The fire is dying away to embers and now I toss carefully crushed nightshade onto them.

Mayhap I am not performing the Rite of Awen in precisely the fashion in which I have seen Myrddin do, nor am I completely certain what I am doing, but I think that I have the gist of it right. And I feel that I am doing it correctly.

I sit before the embers and stare at the softly glow coals.

Lightning wreathes one of the distant mountains in harsh light. Its jagged peak is lost in the clouds, but it bears a strong resemblance to a fang.

The peaceful aura of the ritual is gone now, replaced by a sense of foreboding.

* * *

"We must make haste," I announce to Livia the next morning as I enter her bedchamber and throw back the blankets which cover her nude limbs.

She curses me and grasps blindly for the blankets. "'Tis early yet." She has her eyes squeezed shut against the sunlight pouring through the half-open shutters.

"'Tis almost noon."

"As I said, 'tis early yet." She stops flailing her arms, and glares balefully at me.

I smile at her.

"I had wondered where thou had gotten thyself off too," she tells me as she finally rolls herself out of the bed and pulls a dress from where it has been casually discarded atop a wooden chest. "Thou has been missing all night and half of the day before."

"I was out of town, conducting another ritual."

"Gods," she moans as she finishes adjusting the fall of her gown, "thou are now becoming a proper sorcerer." Disdaining her usual face paints and jewelry, she follows me into the corridor. She shakes her head as the door closes behind her. "How long before thou take up the white robes of Celtic priest?"

"I shall not go quite so far."

"Thy steps have been set for thee." Haakon steps around the corner of the hallway and gazes at us both. "As I expected."

"Livia, this is Haakon, a seer." I hasten to make introductions and mask my own sudden confusion. I had not sensed Haakon's approach. "Haakon, this is the Lady Livia Auerillius, my companion of the roads." Even now, he seems muted to my senses despite my focus.

"The Dark Lady," he says calmly. "The Queen of Sorrows."

She looks startled by the name.

"Had another vision?" I inquire of him. "Or just been listening to the servants gossip?"

"Another sorcerer...thou gods, is everyone taking up spell casting?" Livia asks loudly of the ceiling.

"Who be spell casting?" Siggardson demands as he rounds the corner of the corridor. "Be there some fresh and true word of the necromancer preying on the town below?" His left hand gropes at his side for a nonexistent sword while his left hand tightens on his walking stick.

"No one here practices the dark arts, Guvenor Siggardson." Haakon makes that statement with a confident, calming tone. "But Franc and his lady friend shall be leaving us soon, for they must be at their journey's end ere November Eve."

"They are?"

"We are?"

"Yes, Livia, we are. We have to head into the mountains." I know the one where we shall at least start our search for the Talisman in earnest. "Our quest leads us there to the Fang."

She is staring at me. "Thou have learned something?" she guesses.

I nod carefully. "I am called into the mountains, by a power and means which I cannot divine.

Ye, however, retain numerous options. Thou could no doubt remain here in Hedeby with Guvenor Siggardson as his honoured guest. Or thou could seek out a ship in the harbor which could ferry thou back to the warm southlands." I allow myself the brief hope that she will choose a wise option and leave me to finish this alone.

A moment later, I know my wish is a futile one, for she is looking directly into my eyes with the fierce expression of a hawk sighting a mouse. "Fine, I shall make myself ready to sally forth." She casts a quick look down at her loose-fitting dress. "I be not dressed for an excursion in this climate.

Mayhap I should avail myself of the local fashions and shop before we depart."

"Aye, it would be a wise choice of thine, my Lady." Siggardson is quite happy to offer her his arm. "Indeed, 'tis a far wiser choice of thine to stay here in my hall than journey forth into the wilds of the mountains in this season. 'Tis no place for a lady."

I look at Haakon's serene face with a fierce expression as Siggardson leads Livia deeper into his hall. "What can thou tell me about mountains?" I ask him. "Specifically the one which rears its fang-like crest to the northeast...."

Chapter Fifteen

We ride into the snow-shrouded mountains.

We have left the bustling town of Hedeby many leagues behind us, and make our slow way through the harsh lands of the north. Siggardson proved kind-hearted for he sold us two horses at little cost, a fraction of what we expected to pay in the open marketplace. Livia claims credit for his generosity; "Few mortal men can resist my charms," she reminds me at every opportunity. We follow a road, a packed-hard track of dirt which wends its way northeast, towards the mountain which the locals call Ymir's Tooth. Despite Livia's misgivings and complaints, we ride mostly by day and make camp just after when the sun begins to sink. The sunlight is weak here in the north and even Livia, well-wrapped within her cloak and slathered with my herbal lotions, can make little true complaint about travelling by its wan light. The days are short as well, but even we with our super-human strength cannot ride constantly. Nor can our borrowed horses keep up such a pace for long. The track itself is strewn with hazards, such as fallen stones and sink holes, which further slow our pace for the safety of our horses. As we slowly climb the slope of one of the region's smaller mountains, the soil becomes noticeably poorer and the trees grow stunted by wind and cold.

"Such a desolate place," Livia comments as we stand at a crossroads of sorts. The main path, worn fairly smooth by endless years of traffic curves to the east now, skirting the slopes of the mountain. A rougher track, choked with scraggly and sickly weeds appears to climb the mountain towards its peak. Our horses stand waiting for us to decide which path to follow. My steed paws at the road and neighs softly.

"Aye, 'tis that indeed." As far as I can see, the land is barren. Even the stunted trees have given way to low grasses and lichen-covered rocks.

"I have not seen a sign of habitation in leagues and leagues." She gestures to the emptiness around us and then draws her cloak more tightly around her slender form. "Not a single farm since we left Hedeby behind us."

"This is a harsh land." And an ill-omened one, from what Haakon had told me. "Few of the peasants hereabouts seek to farm the soil. 'Tis not suited for crops." I recall the words of the old seer.

"Haakon said that this land was cursed by the Witch King."

"It appears to have been cursed by someone." Livia's lip curls in a sneer. "The port was rich enough, but less than five leagues from the sea, the land be barren of life

"Barren of mortals, aye."

"And of other things." She gestures again. "Have thou heard the song of birds or the cry of small animals?"

I shake my head.

"Precisely!"

"I have seen some field mice."

"Those were rats and foxes."

"Siggardson himself warned us that few travelers use this road, despite its appearance."

I nod in agreement with her. "Aye, we have seen no other travelers for days."

"Most traffic to Hedeby comes and leaves by ship. The few merchants who do travel by caravan tend to follow the coastline."

"The bulk of the settlements are placed along the coast. Near to the sea which features strongly in the local culture. Close to fish and fresh water and slightly less mountainous lands."

A raven chooses that exact moment to caw.

"A bird," I point out triumphantly.

"A raven," she agrees. We both stare into the sky, seeking to spot the lone bird. "A carrion eater."

"Thy pardon? A carrion eater, thou say?"

"Aye, Franc. The rats and the ravens be eaters of the dead." She shivers. "Even these plants look to be half-dead as they grow. They be but stunted, pathetic things." She plucks a weed from the grass and it crumbles into dust in her hand. "The only thing to have power around here is death."

"Then mayhap we be upon the proper track."

"The Talisman be a thing of death?"

"The scroll said ' the Talisman which gives life to those deceased, be hidden within the desolation of the Wyrm. ' And this," I gesture grandly to the desolate landscape, "is certainly not a natural thing." I would swear that these plants are rotting even as they still try to grow. "Can't thou smell it?"

"Aye." Livia wrinkles her nose. "The scent of corruption be thick upon the wind."

"And the wind blows from the northeast.

"Aye." The cold wind tugs at her wolf fur-lined cloak. "I trust that thou are certain of thy path?" she says as she adjusts her cloak around herself.

"Of course I am." I allow just a hint of anger to colour my words. "I fail to see why I should have to answer to thee, Livia. If thou do not trust me to guide thou to the Talisman, then mayhap thou should seek it on thy own!"

She straightens her back, pulling herself up in a haughty fashion.

I glare directly at her, matching her haughtiness.

She sniffs, then smiles wanly. "I trust ye," she says in a calmer tone. "I have little choice in the matter after all." She nods her head to me and smiles more widely.

I smile back at her, calming the sudden rage. I know not whence it has come, but the long journey we have been on is most likely the cause. We two have seldom seen eye-to-eye and tempers between our Kind tend to flare with sudden violence more often than not. We are solitary predators, not pack hunters. "Then we ride to the crest of Ymir's Tooth, if we must." I shake the reins of my steed. "We ride!"

Boulders begin to line the path as we start our climb up the slope of Ymir's Tooth. A recent snow covers the ground and the hooves of our horses break through the crust with sharp cracks.

I glance back over my shoulder at a sound. A fall of rock? Is that a hint of a black cloak vanishing behind a boulder, or just my imagination?

Livia gives no sign of having seen or heard anything so I dismiss the incident from my mind.

We round a corner on the path, a spur of jagged rock looming above us and forcing us, and the path we follow, to curve around its bulk.

I look back over my shoulder. We stand high on the slope now and I can see for what seems like hundreds of leagues across the land. A low ridge hides the sea from my eyes.

"Do thou know whence thou travel?" Livia calls to me. Her horse kicks at a small rock and neighs loudly.

"I am drawn northward."

"We are running out of northward if thou insist upon climbing this accursed mountain."

"We are close."

"Thou sound certain."

"I feel something nearby. A thing of power." A great power. A dark and shadowy power lurking in the back of my mind.

We move further, picking our way between large boulders and deep fissures in the black rock.

At this height, there is no dirt, nor even lichen clinging to the rock of the mountain.

"This be the place!"

Livia reins in her horse at my shout.

I stare at the canyon. Some old fissure in the rocks has lost its roof to the elements and now gapes open to the sky. I dismount from my steed and hurriedly walk into the canyon. The walls rise up above me, thrice my height. The ground is soft, a fine layer of dirt cushioning the rocks.

"'Tis almost impressive."

I ignore her comment. "'Tis a place of beauty," I reply. "Harsh and unyielding, and yet there is a feeling to it. An aura."

"Thy auras are becoming annoying."

I pace across the open ground. The canyon mouth is narrow, a few paces wide, but the roughly square interior gapes twenty paces or more at its widest. My cloak swirls as I spin on my heel to survey my surroundings again. The rocks are jagged and sharp, strewn with boulders and outcroppings. Splotches of sickly yellow-green lichen cling to a handful of places.

"Now this is interesting." Livia is staring at one of the walls. "See here, Franc? The rest of the walls be rough and yet this area be smooth." She runs her fingertips lightly along the rock. "Very smooth, as if polished." She turns to me with a frown. "How is this possible?"

A wide smile adorns my face. "This be the place!"

Chapter Sixteen

November Eve has come to us at last. The full moon is slowly rising above the mountains and midnight draws ever closer

"This is the key time when the Veil between the Otherworld and this World weaken and thin away almost to nothingness, thus allowing easy travel between the two realms." I smile happily at Livia. "This is the right place for us to be."

She looks up at the cliff-face rising before us. "Are thou certain?" she asks.

"Of course. I can feel that we are in the right place. And at the right time as well, my Lady." I glance back over my shoulder. The canyon in which we are standing is roughly square, with almost-sheer walls rising to thrice our height. The moon is just visible, cresting the top of the canyon. "It should be directly overhead by midnight." I have become a master of judging the passage of the moon and the stars.

"And what of the fog?" she asks me calmly.

I glance down at the faint wisps of pale mist gathering around our boots. "I do not think it will cause us trouble in this casting." The mist puzzled me though. I would have sworn that the temperature was far too cold for any mist to gather. "And yet here it is," I murmur too softly for my companion to overhear.

"I trust in thy judgement, Franc." Livia eyes the cliff again, scanning the sheer rock face. She draws the well-made green cloak more tightly around her body. Even on this night, she has forgone her favored dresses for a tunic and breeches of a thick and warm cloth. "I see no opening." There is grey fur lining her cloak as well. 'Tis from a wolf, I think.

"It will appear. At the proper time." I strive to sound confident though I am doing little more than guessing wildly. "Come, we must finish our preparations." I lead Livia from the canyon back to our small campsite. The mountain, Ymir's Tooth, looms over us. "The herbs must be ground before they can be cast onto the fire." A gust of wind brings a foul scent to my nose. I sneeze.

Livia doesn't even look at me as she digs through our saddlebags for the appropriate herbs.

"Soon it shall be within our grasp!" she sighs aloud. "Soon we have ultimate power over the mortal world!"

"We shall see." I feel constrained to point that fact out to her. "Not all prophecies mean precisely what we expect them too."

"When do thou cast thy spell?" she asks, dismissing my warning.

"Midnight will be the most potent time for the casting to take place." Noting that Livia has yet to find the herbs, I reach towards my own saddlebags.

"Yes, midnight will be precisely the proper time," Ulric announces as he steps from behind a large boulder. His black cloak hangs from his shoulders and further obscures his body within the moon-cast shadows. "And with the rising fog, we be blessed with a double Threshold, a truly good sign."

Livia's mouth is hanging open as she stares at our unwelcome visitor. She looks scared.

Confusion and shock mingle in her scent, along with a surprising amount of fear.

I reach for my sword, masking my own fear. "I do not know how thou have returned here, Witch King, but this time thou shall not survive my wrath!"

Ulric chuckles as brawny Norsemen step into sight from behind other boulders and stunted trees and carefully aim their bows at us. "Do not prove troublesome, Franc, lest thy maiden-friend be slain before thy eyes." His smile is ghastly, a wide tooth-filled grin by a face devoid of spare flesh. He looks like an animated skeleton more than a living man. "And thee as well," he adds with a growing grin. "I have taken great care to dip the tips of our arrows into a potion of my own brewing...it should prove fatal even to a being of thy special Kind."

"This be not possible!" Livia protests.

"I know," I agree with her. "He should be dead! I drained him myself." My eye falls on Sven, standing near Ulric's side with a huge axe in his hands. He looks eager for us to resist, and I have no doubt that he can use that axe to chop a man in twain with a single swing.

"Do thou wish to test my patience further?" Ulric demands. His cloak stirs in the sudden chill wind. "Continue to delay and thou shall taste the potency of my potions for thyself."

I eye the archers. How many arrows can I dodge? Two? A dozen? A score? He has at least two scores of Norsemen standing ready to attack us. "Damn."

"I have no more time to linger with ye. Surrender, or thou both die."

Grimly, I lower my sword. "Thou win," I tell him. "For now," I add in a faint whisper as the Norsemen close in around us.

We are forced to kneel, our hands bound behind our backs with stout ropes, and other ropes are tied from our necks to a spear driven firmly into the ground. The ropes, though seeming of a coarse weave, are well-made, for neither Livia nor I can break them despite our best struggles.

Sven grins down at us, clearly amused by our futile struggles.

"This be a most auspicious day," Ulric tells us as his followers prepare for the ritual to come.

"A Grove Day—Samhain no less—with a full moon, a rising fog, and perchance a lightning storm?" His eyes gleam brightly in the moonlight. "'Tis many of the most potent Threshold Times blending together...and thus intensifying their power and influence far beyond their natural strengths. This ritual tonight will succeed." He waves his arms, his cloak blowing in the wind. "It must succeed!"

Livia's eyes are fixed on him as he paces the rocky ground before us. "How can he be here?"

she hisses to me. Her cloak hangs loosely on her, its hood had been pulled down earlier so that the rope could be tied around her neck and has not been replaced.

"Apparently he be not as dead as I had rashly thought." I stare at Ulric with narrowed eyes. I had drained him of blood—surely he cannot be here now!

"Nay, I be not dead. I be immortal, as a god!" Ulric cups Livia's chin in his hand and turns her face so that she is staring up at him. I can only marvel at the strength in those bony fingers. "'Twas a valiant attempt of thee to slay me at the Keep, Man of Gaul, yet thou have failed." His face is even thinner and more skeletal than when I had seen him before. "For with my powers and wisdom I brewed a most potent herbal draught in the days of my youth. I have fought back the very lures of death itself!" A hint of madness lurks within his eyes. "I awoke in that charnel pit whence I had been consigned and struggled my way free of the corpses therein. A lesser man might have gone mad, to awake and find himself imprisoned in such a place, but I be made of stronger stuff."

"And now thou follow us, like a lost puppy."

"Nay, not lost for I have also gained insight into the Talisman I seek. The gods have fated me the right to join them, else all of my servants would have fled Normandy following the battle at Keep Harfleur...and yet I found a single ship waiting at the beach for my return. A loyal crew, waiting to serve me." He gestures to the men around us and gold glints on his fingers. "I am content with the state of events now, for I am on the very edge of seizing my destiny."

Several Norsemen appear out of the thickening fog, like wraiths answering Ulric's call. They hurry past us, carrying firewood into the canyon and stacking it on the ground.

"I have tracked thou carefully, Man of Gaul." Ulric's hand dips within his cloak and then his fingers part to reveal a glimmering bluish crystal sphere cupped therein.

"A scrying stone." Now things were beginning to making sense to me. "I could feel thou watching me."

"I had feared that thou would. Thy Kind possess certain powers in the mystical realms." Ulric returns the scrying stone to his pocket. "But no matter, for I am still well ahead of thee."

"Thy followers will not be able to save ye!"

He looks at Livia. "I need them not. With the Talisman, I shall summon back my followers of old, and my powers will become absolute!" His voice raises to an alarming pitch at that. "I will see my fortress rebuilt and my armies will once again enforce my will upon this land." He whirls on his heel. "And this time I shall not content myself with merely dominating the Norselands, oh no!" He turns to face us once again, and I barely manage to avoid shying away from the naked hatred on his face. "This time, I shall extend my powers and dominance over the entire world!"

"'Tis good to have some small ambition," Livia tells him.

He glares at her. "'Tis almost time for the ritual to begin...I must prepare myself for it would not do to be late." Giggling, the Witch King strides away into the night.

"This be not good," Livia tells me in a low tone.

"Nay, it be not." I sigh and try once again to break the bonds which hold me.

Chapter Seventeen

Freed from the spear, though not from the ropes binding our wrists behind our backs, Livia and I are led by our leashes into the canyon where we are once again forced to kneel on the frozen ground before stacked firewood. I am confident that I could easily slay the few guards holding us here, but I know not how many other Norsemen are gathering nearby. Nor do I wish to test Ulric's foul potion should I be wounded by an arrow or a treated spear.

The Norsemen gather around us in a big circle. Two particularly brawny specimens take positions at my shoulders, standing with drawn swords held ready in their hands.

"Apple wood…difficult to find in these climes," Ulric says with a chuckle as he approaches the stack. "But well worth the effort to gather, methinks, for a ritual of this importance." He gestures to the stacks of wood and chants softly. "Cum Saxum Saxorum. Induersum montum oparium da—In Aetibulum, In Quinatum, Draconis!" Flames crackle to life, blazing away merrily as if they mean to burn forever. "And the appropriate herbs of course, to set the mood and enhance the environment." He tosses herbs into the fire. "Wormwood, nightshade, and ghost flower."

"I am pleased to know that thou came prepared." I can feel a sharp rock digging into my knee but I refuse to shift position, refuse to acknowledge the pain. It helps to focus me.

"What few herbs and ritual necessities I failed to acquire in Hedeby are easily found in thy saddlebags," Ulric sneers at me. "'Tis easier for me to simply take what I need from thou after thou proved kind enough to gather such things together." Smoke mingles with the fog and swirls around us.

"Shall we split the cost of those herbs between us then?" Ulric's glare is worth the pain of the slap which one of his minions gives me.

"Keep silent, Man of Gaul, ere thou lose thy tongue." The Witch King turns on his heel and strides away from us. He waves at his assembled followers. "Begin!" he shouts.

"Anail Nathrock. Uthas Bethudd. Dochiel Dienve," the assembled Norsemen chant in unison.

"Anail Nathrock. Uthas Bethudd. Dochiel Dienve!"

Ulric raises his hands and shouts: "A elfyntodd dwyr sinddyn duw. Cerrig yr fferllurg nwyn; os syriaeth ech saffear tu fewr mor, necrmber blum!"

The wind whips around us, clawing at our garments and hair.

"Erce, erce, erce!" Ulric calls out. "I invoke ye, Powers of Earth, Kingdom of Stone! Behold, Falias, Morfessas, Chobas!" He raises his right hand and traces out a doorway with his index finger.

I recognize the symbol as Trilithon, the Arches. The Witch King is going to conduct the sacred ceremony in my place.

Ulric nods.

One of the Norsemen falls silent and then draws his dagger. He pauses a moment, then raises the blade and scores a deep cut into his right palm. He does not make a single sound as he inflicts the injury. He calmly walks to the face of the cliff as Ulric continues to chant and smears his bloody hand along the rocks, drawing a rough mark with his own blood.

"The rune for opening," I whisper to Livia. "Thorn."

"Opening of what?" she asks me.

"A gateway of some kind I dare think." Another gust of wind blows through the canyon, tugging at our cloaks and setting the fire to flickering. I believe it to be impossible, but the wind seems to be blowing from the cliff face! 'Tis some trick or illusion.

"Erce, erce, erce! I invoke ye, Powers of Earth, Kingdom of Stone! Behold, Falias, Morfessas, Chobas!" Ulric shouts and waves his arms in a grand fashion. "Erce, erce, erce! I invoke ye, Powers of Earth, Kingdom of Stone! Behold, Falias, Morfessas, Chobas!" The wind whips through his hair and tugs at his cloak, though he seems to take no notice.

The chanting Norsemen fell silent.

Ulric stares at the solid wall of rock. "It is here...it must be here!" The chill wind gusts around us, blowing the fog into tatters.

"Having problems?" I ask him with mocking concern.

"Silence," he snarls at me. "Thy time will come." His bony fingers clench into fists of rage, though his wrath is impotent.

"He failed then?" Livia asks me in a scornful voice meant to carry across the gathering.

"Typical then...of what use is a sorcerer unable to succeed at even the simplest of spells?"

"Apparently of little use," I agree.

"I have not failed!" As Ulric gestures, Sven hefts a wooden cask in his hand. "I will not be denied!" Ulric waves his hands violently towards the cliffs one more time. "Erce, erce, erce! I invoke ye, Powers of Earth, Kingdom of Stone! Behold, Falias, Morfessas, Chobas! Erce, erce, erce! I invoke ye, Powers of Fire, Kingdom of Flame! Behold, Finias, Uscias, Dyinas!" As the last word echoes, Sven throws the cask at the rocks.

A thunderous explosion shakes the ground and sulphurous smoke billows thickly around us.

The foul-smelling cloud only slowly vanishes, being blown away by the wind.

A jagged tunnel gapes open, amid broken rocks.

Ulric turns to face us with a wide smile twisting his face. "I told thou that the entrance lay concealed here." His eyes are burning with unholy light. The light of madness. "And now we might go forth that I might seize my destiny!"

His men hastily kindle torches from the smoldering fire.

"What I seek lays within that tunnel, deep under the mountain."

"In its heart?" I call out.

"Aye, within its very heart!" Ulric agrees. "Does that worry thee, Man of Gaul? I know all that thou know about the Talisman and, indeed, I know more."

"Not at all."

Ulric snorts loudly. "Bring the wench," he gestures towards Livia. "Her blood I shall have need of as an offering to the Guardian of the Talisman."

Livia's head snaps around so that she can stare at me. "Thou told me nothing of any guardian!"

she protests. "Lest of all of having to make a blood offering!"

"I did not know of one," I reply. "I don't recall reading about one in any of the scrolls." Maybe I had not read enough. Maybe the Guardian had just been left out by the scribe.

Two more blond Norsemen approach us. Are all Norsemen fair-haired I wonder? One cuts the rope around Livia's neck, and then he and his companion pick her up between them and carry her, with her hands still bound, towards the tunnel's mouth.

"Let me go!" she curses at them. "I can walk myself. Remove thy hands from my person at once!" Her voice recedes as she is carried out of sight.

"Leave her alone!" I shout.

"Silence, Man of Gaul, else I might decide to leave thee here." Ulric pauses, giving that thought another mulling, but then he shakes his head reluctantly. "Nay, I shall take thee along for now.

But know this, for in the first moment that thou cause me trouble, then I shall consider the choice made and thy head shall be hewn from thy body." He nods and two of his minions pull me to my feet, cutting the rope which has bound me to the spear.

I stretch out my neck, working to loosen a kinked muscle.

"Bring him." Ulric strides into the tunnel with a pleased grin upon his face. "Let him bear witness to my ascension to godhood before he dies. The light of madness is truly bright within his eyes.

Chapter Eighteen

The tunnel is roughly hewn from the mountain, with still-jagged rocks forming the walls, countless sharp points ready to snag equally roughly at any loose clothing or unwary flesh which chanced to brush against them. The air is damp, our breath forms mist as we breath, and there is no talking from anyone. The only sound I can hear is the tread of our booted feet on the rocks and the crackle of our flickering torches.

To my own personal amusement, Ulric is forced to walk bent over, as are most of his men, due to the low ceiling. I, again to my amusement, am able to walk almost fully erect, though I move carefully.

More than one of the Witch King's minions, however, gives vent to a heartfelt curse after rubbing against one of the dagger-sharp outcroppings. I can scent blood in the air, mingling with the smoke from the torches. 'Tis enough to cause my stomach to growl. No one takes any notice. I walk carefully; with my arms still bound behind my back, I will be unable to catch myself should I stumble and fall.

At last the tunnel opens out into a large cavern, with a ceiling high enough for all the Norsemen to stand erect once again.

I scan my captors quickly. All of them are present—I had hoped that some few might have been left behind in the tunnel, but no such luck had been given to me from the gods.

"The heart of the stone lays that way," Ulric gestures to the far wall of the cavern. He takes a dozen strides across the ground, skirting a stalagmite.

"Through solid rock, how convenient," Livia's voice echoes clearly back to me.

She smells irritated, and I do not sense any hint of pain from her. Clearly she did not brush against the rocks during the trek through the tunnel. I am impressed. From what I recall, she had never enjoyed cramped spaces and that tunnels surely is confining. Of course, she is still bound so that might also explain her temper.

"There be other ways to travel there. This mountain be filled with many tunnels and caverns. A veritable rabbit's warren."

"And thou be the weasel?"

Ulric's mouth thins as he glares at her. "Gag her."

"Thank you."

The look Livia casts at me when I speak is murderous, yet I know that her incessant chatter will hinder, more than help, our cause.

Ulric holds a small bluish crystal upon his right palm and he peers carefully into its depths. His mouth moves in a soundless chant—even I cannot make out what he is saying.

I stare at the crystal. It reminds me of Myrddin's Pelen Tan. Very similar in shape. My eyes narrow. 'Tis very similar.

Ulric slips the crystal back into his pocket. "We go that way." He gestures to another open tunnel, just a few paces to the left of the one from which we just emerged. I had failed to notice it until now. At least this one looks to be of a height sufficient for all to walk through in more comfort than the previous one. "The prisoners will walk near the rear."

Peering about by the light of the torch carried by the guard behind me, I can see that despite the greater height, the walls of this tunnel remain covered with sharp rocks and stalactites. The rocks are veined with minerals, giving them a bright colour.

Other tunnels open from this one. And still others lead elsewhere into the mountain's heart. It is a warren, as Ulric had said, a maze of tunnels and caverns.

From the low murmurs, some of the Norsemen are becoming afraid. I can see the glances they cast about, the manner in which they tighten their grips upon their swords and axes as we pass by those gaping tunnel mouths. I can only smile. They fear the darkness which lays heavily around us like some ominous shroud. Anything could be lurking within this mountain, lairing within the tunnels, waiting for prey to stumble blindly into reach.

I turn to share the joke with Livia, and feel surprise at the fact that she is eyeing the tunnels with an unusual degree of nervousness. I can scent it from her.

My eyes narrow.

Mayhap there are things lairing here to make even my Kind afraid?

Ulric is the only one who does not seem to be in the least affected by the darkness of the tunnels. He maintains his steady pace, wandering deeper and deeper into the heart. He strides past most of the alternate tunnels, pausing only now and then to briefly consult his scrying stone.

I think that we are journeying southward through the tunnels, but I am no longer clear of our direction. The tunnels twist and curve in such a way that I am certain we are traveling as much sideways as we are forward.

* * *

The walls of the cavern are very gradually becoming less rough.

They appear to have been carved and roughly smoothed, hewn from the living rock by ancient builders. "Mayhap Dwarves," I tell Livia after shifting my position within the ranks of the Norsemen so that I might walk beside her. Our captors take no note of our movements, save that we keep pace with them. Indeed, now that I look closer at the walls, I can even make out the brackets where ancient torches were once set upon the walls.

And then we reach the stairs.

The stairs lead downwards, deeper into the earth. The steps are spaced rather oddly for humans, much too short for most of Ulric's men to use comfortably. Far too short for Ulric himself, who grumbles softly as he descends them by torchlight.

I ponder the mystery as I make my way carefully down the spiral. Each step is scarcely half the height of a normal one, and only half as deep. 'Tis interesting, and more than sufficient evidence for me to conclude that the stairs were carved by Dwarves.

Well, either Dwarves or Trolls.

I dismiss that thought at once. Trolls are not known for their tunneling work and they would never have carved such a tight spirally stairwell. No, a Troll cave would be more rough and of course, there would be the stench of unwashed Troll in the air. The dampness of the cave, though dank, does not bear the stench of Troll.

It does not smell of Dwarf either.

The steps end in a circular cavern, and yet another dark tunnel leads deeper into shadow-cloaked mystery. The brackets on these walls hold torches. Kindled torches.

I glance at Livia who looks back at me in confusion. How long have those torches been there, to be burning still? Was there someone—or something—to tend them?

There are symbols etched into the rocks above the cavern.

"Runes," Ulric says in a low voice. He is speaking mostly to himself, but I can hear him clearly. "Runes carved by ancient hands." He chuckles and holds his torch closer to them. "But still quite readable."

"Any fool can read runes," I tell him in a loud voice. Several of the Norsemen mutter and eye me cautiously, for most of them cannot read, although they recognize the runes for what they are.

"Then read the message," Ulric orders me with a mocking tone. "Prove thy knowledge to us then."

"I might need better light." In truth, the light from the flickering torches is bright enough, but I feel the perverse need to annoy the Witch King as much as possible.

"Read!" Ulric is not amused.

"I see the runes of Yr and Ealh. Defense and Protection. I also see a rune meaning the Unknowable. "

"Wyrd." Ulric gestures to the runes with his torch. "This be the place…'Let ye, whomever dare to approach, be warned that Thou who seek the prize must know that there be a terrible price to pay.'

'Tis simple enough to decipher." His pleased chuckle echoes through the tunnel and up the stairs.

"This be the place!" he cries out happily, thrusting his fists towards the ceiling in triumph. "The talisman be mine!" His triumphant shout echoes.

A rumbling sound issues forth from the tunnel ahead.

A few of the Norsemen mutter softly and their take a firmer grip upon their weapons.

"I will have my dues before this night has ended." Ulric smiles, his lips pulling away from his sharp teeth. "I will have what is rightfully mine." Abruptly he takes note of the muttering from his gathered minions. "Silence louts!" he snaps. "There do not be anything to fear."

"But the guardian?" one of the Norsemen protests.

"Will not trouble us. I will placate him." He sounds supremely confident.

"Offer him gold and jewels you mean?" I ask aloud. "Or just give him eternal life?"

"I would grant thee eternal life," Ulric tells me in a harsh voice, "if only to allow me time enough to make thee suffer sufficiently from the torments which I wish to bestow upon thee." He turns back towards the tunnel, obviously feeling the pull of something beyond the tunnel's mouth. "I lack such time, alas, so thy death will be swift, mostly painless, and final."

"I see."

"Karl, Alexandre. Kill him for me. I must go forth to claim my prize and deal with the mysterious guardian." Ulric turns and strides into the dark tunnel, the majority of his Norsemen following him. And dragging Livia with them I note.

My two captors watch the others go and then turn towards me. Their faces show no emotion.

"Ruuskin?" I ask them. "Or Germanic? Thou do not be Norse by thy names." Neither of them answer me, save to glower at me darkly. "Can we talk this over?" I ask as they stare at me with baleful expressions.

Karl draws his axe and hefts it with both hands. The blade looks very sharp.

"I will take that as a no then." I glance at Alexandre who is also taking a firm grip on his axe.

"Then we must do this the hard way." I duck the first swing.

Karl is taken by surprise and stumbles forward, put off-balance by my sudden movement.

I twist around and lift my arms just enough that the still-swinging axe blade catches the ropes binding my wrists and slices them in half. My smile widens. "I thank ye." I grab Alexandre's axe as he swings at me and pull him forward sharply. I swing the axe around my own body and smash the Norseman into the cavern wall. He slumps to the ground with a moan. The bloody wound on his forehead is nasty and I do not think that he will awaken from it.

Karl has regained his balance and now he lunges at me again with a growl.

I raise the shaft of my stolen axe and block his blow with it. Sparks fly from the blades as they meet with a clang.

"Thou shall have to do better than that," I tell him. The axe is heavy, though not too burdensome for me—with my unnatural strength. But if these two mortals are swinging them around with such ease, then I know that these are well-skilled warriors indeed.

I strike out again and then sidestep Karl's return blow. From the look on his face, I can tell that he knows he has been bested. I make my final swing.

The axe blade tears deep into his chest and he drops to his knees with a gasp. His eyes look at me with tangible hatred, until he topples over.

I leave the axe in his chest and draw my dagger. Looks like it will be up to me to save Livia and then the rest of the world.

Chapter Nineteen

I hurry through the tunnel, my eyes easily able to see despite the lack of torches here.

Everything is tinged in shades of blue, the night-vision a gift of my Kind, and vaguely blurry, as if I look through a fog. The tunnel twists and curls through the mountain, very much like the rabbit warren which Ulric had earlier compared it to. I have no choice but to follow the main shaft, hoping that my quarry did not turn down some side passage.

I can hear voices from up ahead echoing back to me faintly.

Ulric is chanting softly, the Charm of Making I think as I hear the words "Dochiel Dienve"

echoing to my ears . He must be readying himself for further magick, summoning his powers to him.

I pick up my pace, hurrying forward through the tunnel. The sounds of my boots on the rocky ground are soft and I doubt that Ulric or any of his band will hear my approach over the sounds of their own passage.

Livia, however, might and take comfort in knowing that I am still alive.

Faint reddish light can just be seen from ahead of me.

The thought strikes me that even if the Norsemen have posted sentries and hear my approach, they will likely assume me to be Alexandre and Karl.

I slow as I approach the bend in the tunnel. Ulric and his company are using torches and the light is, strangely enough, welcome to me after the oppressive darkness of the endless tunnels. How long since we left the world above to descend into the depths of the earth? Hours or days? And why does this shadowy place feel so wrong to me? I carefully peer around the corner.

The cavern they stand in has a tall ceiling, hung with many red-streaked stalactites. Ulric has moved apart from his men, pacing away from them across the soft ground. They are murmuring softly.

I do not see Livia. There is a strong stench of decay which makes even me wrinkle my nose. For a moment, I think that I can smell trolls. But no, this loathsome stench is too foul and strong even for those vermin.

Ulric is moving towards what looks to be a flight of steps carved into a particularly squat stalagmite. Something glitters atop the rock.

The glitter catches my eye...the lichen which grows on the rocks and walls is glowing a pale green, which gives everyone's skin an unhealthy tinge.

I step forward, out of the tunnel. And look down in surprise as my boots sink into mud. The cavern floor is like the edge of a marsh, soft and boggy. I pull my boots free and carefully squelch my way towards Ulric.

"The talisman!" Ulric calls out. "I can see it at last!"

So can I, after I squint just a bit.

The talisman is a jewel-encrusted scepter. A pace or so in length, it is tipped by a blood-red ruby carved into a leering skull.

"The Scepter of Hades!" Ulric laughs loudly as he climbs the final few steps towards the dais.

"At long last, immortality is within my grasp!" Grinning widely, he reaches his skeletal hand towards the gleaming rod.

A tremendous roar echoes through the cavern. The ground shakes and shudders and flakes of rock rain down on us from the ceiling.

"The Guardian!" one of the Norsemen shouts and others echo the cry.

Something moves in the shadows which cloak the far side of the cavern. And then the Guardian looms its massive bulk into sight.

A Wyrm.

Even I feel my blood run cold at the sight. The Wyrm resembles a giant snake, of great length, with a pair of taloned claws extending from where its shoulders should be. Its scales are a greenish-yellow colour, slick with a foul-smelling slime.

"A lyndorm," Ulric says, in surprise. He is staring at the beast, his jaw slack and his eyes glazing over. It seems that he has forgotten the Scepter, just beyond his reach, as the Guardian rears up.

The beast roars, opening its fang-filled jaws wide enough to swallow a grown man whole.

"Kill the beast!" Ulric shouts over the mutters of his minions. Dismissing them, he turns back to stare at the Scepter, the object of his quest.

Half a dozen Norsemen charge towards the dragon...and are knocked sprawling by a sudden sweep of its sinuous tail.

Others charge, led by Sven, hacking at the beast with their axes and swords. The lyndorm's scales prove tougher than the blades of men and they cause no apparent harm despite the violence of their blows

They do appear to be angering the beast, though, and it lunges into the midst of the largest crowd, composed of those warriors who have yet to throw themselves into the sudden battle. The dragon is a deadly foe, a natural predator, and it makes full use of its body as a weapon. Clawed feet slice through the chests of hapless Norsemen as easily as a newly-honed knife cuts through soft cheese.

Its mouth snaps at others, biting some.

I see one Norseman reel away from the dragon staring at the bloody stump which had once been his arm.

Another man cries out as a talon cuts apart his stomach allowing him to see his insides spill onto the ground at his feet.

The dragon roars.

"Livia!" I shout. She is in the midst of that brawl, no doubt still tied up and all but helpless. I plunge into the fighting, even as the dragon moves elsewhere, charging at another group of Norsemen who meet it with eager shouts. "Livia, where are you?" Torches lay spluttering on the muddy ground, abandoned by those who had carried them, and now most of the light comes from the sickly glow of the lichen. "Answer me!" I shove one Norseman out of my path and look back as I realize that he is carrying Shadow's Kiss! I snatch my blade from his hand and then duck as the dragon's tail narrowly avoid hitting me.

I se a hint of green cloth under two fallen Norsemen.

"Livia!" I yank one body aside with a grunt.

"Don't scream so much," Livia grumbles as she tries to struggle back to her feet. "Thou givest me a headache."

I cut the ropes binding her wrists with my dagger and help her to stand.

She vainly tries to brush mud and slime from her tunic. "Those louts have not bathed in months methinks." She eyes the dragon as it fights, raising one delicate eyebrow as she studies how swiftly it moves. "I had not expected to see such a beast as that," she comments in a dry tone. Her hand rests on the slender dagger still hanging from her belt. It seems that the Norsemen did not consider her a threat worthy of disarming.

"One dragon versus nearly thirty of Ulric's minions." I smile grimly. "I think the odds favour the dragon."

"I want the Scepter," she tells me in a calm voice. "I want it, Franc." She is staring at Ulric who has halted his ascent to watch the dragon slay his followers. Staring at him hungrily, with naked lust on her face.

"I think the dragon is a bigger concern right now." I heft my sword. Shadow's Kiss is a fine blade, but I am not sure that it is a match for such a beast as the Wyrm.

"Thou handle the dragon then, I will deal with Ulric." Livia begins to pick her way across the muddy ground. "Slaying dragons be no task for a demure lady."

I can scarcely believe her tone. "So thou keep telling me, but I have yet to see overmuch example of thy being a lady, demure or otherwise."

She snorts.

I turn my attention back to the dragon. It is still slaughtering the Norsemen and the Norsemen are still trying to slay it. I have to wonder who is smarter...the beast or the men?

Of course, I can scarcely think ill of them for here I now am, throwing myself into the same fray like a fool.

Well, not quite a fool.

Unlike the Norsemen, I do not blindly charge at the beast screaming loudly and so it does not seem to take notice of me as I approach from behind it.

My first sword blow glances off the scales with a peculiar clanging sound.

The dragon, however, does deign to notice me then and its jaws only narrowly miss snapping my head from my body.

I throw myself from its path and roll across the ground. I hastily scramble back to my feet. My lips part in a sudden grimace. "This is not going to be pleasant," I mutter.

Ulric turns away from the fight. "I hope the beast slays him." His eyes are fixated upon the Scepter. "At last," he sighs. He reaches towards the glittering rod and his skeletally-thin fingers curl around its cold surface. "Mine!" he crows triumphantly above the roars of the dragon and the shouts of his men.

"Mine!" Livia crows as her own delicate fingers wrap around the Scepter.

Both stare at each other. Hatred mingles with astonishment on their faces.

"'Tis mine, wench!"

"The Scepter is mine, Witch King!"

They struggle, standing atop the stalagmite, each grasping at the Scepter with two hands and trying relentlessly to pull the talisman from the other's desperate grip. Their lips pull back from their teeth as they channel more and more of their anger into the impromptu tug-of-war.

I strike at the dragon again, my sword striking hard with every ounce of strength that I can muster. "Come, Shadow's Kiss, prove to me thy worth!"

One of the scales shatters, exposing the beast's softer skin.

"Have at ye!" one of the Norsemen cries out and plunges his spear into the wound I have just made.

The dragon shrieks.

The cavern shudders at the sound and rocks rain down on us. The dragon lashes out and its tail flattens two more hapless warriors. Its talons claim another life, and its jaws narrowly miss claiming me.

"This is madness!" I know not to whom I am speaking, but I feel the urge to say something as the dragon whirls about to seek me.

Its eyes burn with a most baleful light.

A glare similar to that of Ulric, I note idly.

I raise my sword. "Shadow's Kiss can hurt ye, beast. Do thou wish to face my sting again?"

Apparently my blade is truly forged of some superior metal for none of the Norsemen have yet to injure the beast in the slightest.

It roars again. And again.

A falling stalactite crushes a Norseman standing near me.

I rush the beast and strike with my sword. The dragon shrieks as my blade cuts deep into its neck.

The beast topples to the ground with a tremendous crash which flings sticky mud in all directions and shakes the very ground beneath us.

Chapter Twenty

I gasp for breath. A hard fight, but one worthy of song I dare think. If there are any left alive to sing it. My hasty glance reveals me to be the only man yet standing, all others lay broken and still in the mud. I have won. I look up. The Scepter!

Livia and Ulric still vie for possession of the talisman. They are cursing each other and I can hear their words now, in the sudden silence which follows the dragon's death.

"'Tis mine," Ulric hisses. "I will not be denied this right, this destiny." He gives a sudden pull and yanks the Scepter free from Livia's grip. He kicks at her and she tumbles down the steps to the muddy ground below. "At last!" His eyes burns and his sharp teeth are bared in a fearsome smile.

Livia stares up at him, trying to gather strength enough to regain her feet. "So thou have won."

Her voice is bitter, more bitter than rancid lemons. "And look around thee! Thy minions lay slain by the Guardian."

Ulric laughs scornfully at her. "So what if they are?" he demands. "With this," at that he hefts the Scepter, "I can resurrect them all. I can grant them immortality!"

"Thou have thy army," I say as I approach the steps with my sword held ready. "And now what? Thou shall ride forth to conquer the world?"

"Perhaps," Ulric admits, "or mayhap I shall simply ride forth to slaughter and pillage all that I find. I will begin a reign of blood and terror which shall make the fall of Rome seem a tavern brawl."

He waves the Scepter around with his right hand. "With this, I can do anything!" His shout echoes through the cavern. "I am a god!"

"And I pity anyone desperate enough to pray to thee," Livia tells him.

"Anail Nathrock, Uthas Bethudd, Dochiel Dienve." Ulric waves the Scepter from right to left and the ruby skull glitters. "Anail Nathrock, Uthas Bethudd, Dochiel Dienve! Faint light gleam over the hearth!" he calls out. "Ghosts of Arden pass through and show thy distant forms. Misty Lods, House to the Spirits of Men—when ghosts vanish like mists on a sunny hill, open thy doors!"

A chill wind blows through the cavern.

It carries the stench of a freshly dug grave.

"The fool has done it this time," I murmur. "He's summoning forth the spirits of the dead!"

"That is what I planned to do!" Livia reminds me. She has regained her feet and glares up at the Witch King with a fierce expression on her face. "I must have that Scepter," she whispers to me. "I must."

I point my sword at him. "Stop this madness, Ulric! Summoning up the dead will be a mistake!"

"Is it?" Ulric counters. "It is what thou desire, Man of Gaul. A pity that I, not ye, control the Scepter and thus have the power to give life." His eyes glitter with the unholy fire of true madness.

"And to take it, perhaps." He wave his left hand. "In Quinatum, Draconis!" He flicks his hand towards us and a fireball leaps from his fingers.

I bat it aside with my sword.

The flame strikes the ground and erupts into a fierce fire. Even in the slimy mud, it burns violently.

"So, thou wish to play then?" Ulric snarls at us. "So be it. In Quinatum, Draconis!" He throws another fireball at me.

I dodge it as well.

I wonder how the fires are managing to burn on the damp ground. Sorcery, I decide with a shiver.

"Keep him busy," Livia tells me and scurries off to the far side of the stalagmite.

"Thou have been abandoned by thy friends," Ulric tells me as he rains down fireballs which I only just manage to keep dodging. "A grave pity for thee."

"At least I have friends," I mock.

"Friends are weak," Ulric counters. "Better to be served than to have others expecting thou to serve them in turn. The Christian Devil said it best, methinks. For I find that it is indeed far better to reign in Hell than to serve in Heaven!"

"Thou can discuss such with him then, when I send thou to meet him in person." I place my boot upon the first step of the stalagmite.

"Draconis!" Ulric gesture at the roughly carved steps and flames rise up between him and me.

I stand in place and simply stare at the wall of flame in surprise. What could be feeding the flames? Solid rock simply does not burn like dried and aged wood and yet the heat of the conflagration is sharp on my face.

"Thou struggle with such determination to oppose me, Man of Gaul, and yet now thou are little more than an insect to me. A worm on his belly crawling in the mud and thinking that the slime is thy entire world."

"I am not beaten yet."

"True, but I can change that." Ulric waves the Scepter again and begins to chant. "Faint light gleam over the hearth! Ghosts of Arden pass through and show thy distant forms. Misty Lods, House to the Spirits of Men—when ghosts vanish like mists on a sunny hill, open thy doors!"

I ascend to the second stair, drawing closer to the flames.

Then I hear the moans.

I twist my head around to stare back into the cavern.

The fallen Norsemen are rising painfully to their feet. Unsteadily, they begin to stagger towards me.

I can see blood slowly oozing from the fatal wounds that killed them. I can smell the rot and decay already setting into their bones. I cannot hear them breathing though.

"My army arises!" Ulric crows. "Come to me, my Resurrected! Serve me and slay this bold hero who would dare to oppose my destiny!"

I eye the living corpses with disbelief. Such is not what I had expected. This is the resurrection promised? This is the fate far worse than death of which many have spoken. 'Tis the very Hell the Christians preach about.

The first warrior reaches me and I stab him with my sword, ducking his own axe as it swings towards me.

The fact that he does not fall proves to be only a mild surprise to me. I am becoming jaded, methinks.

He makes no sound as he continues to attack me. Quickly, I slice the head from atop his neck with my next blow and still the body does not stop trying to hew me with his axe. At least the man is slow, moving like a greybeard of eighty summers. But he has many friends who are slowly drawing near. And all of them are as silent as the grave.

"Victory is mine, Man of Gaul. There be nothing thou can do to stop me." Ulric stares at the gleaming Scepter clenched in his hand. The skull glitters brightly, burning with an inner fire.

"Nothing."

"Franc be resourceful," Livia says as she snatches the Scepter from Ulric's hand, "as am I."

Ulric stares at her for a moment with his mouth hanging open in shock.

Even as I desperately fight against the Resurrected, I allow myself a moment of surprise that Livia has been able to scale the stalagmite unaided.

"And now the power of eternal life is mine!" Livia holds the Scepter aloft in her hand. "I shall take a place among the gods!" Her eyes are shining with what I can only assume is a madness equal to Ulric's own.

"No!" Ulric shouts and grabs at the Scepter.

Again the two begin to struggle for control of the talisman.

I am relieved when the horde of undead warriors halt their unsteady advance towards me and simply stand still, swaying gently on their feet. They are still silent, staring blankly at nothing with their glazed eyes.

The silence is the worst part!

"Faint light gleam over the hearth!" Ulric begins to chant in a harsh voice. "Ghosts of Arden pass—"

"Would thou shut up!" Livia screeches at him. "I have heard enough of thy babbling!" She lets go of the Scepter with one hand and punches the Witch King in the face.

He lets go of the Scepter in surprise and stumbles backwards a step. He gives his head a quick shake to clear it and then he bares his teeth and lunges at her with a fierce snarl.

Even as Livia lifts the Scepter in triumph, Ulric raises a small dagger and plunges it into her breast.

She cries out, startled more than hurt, and the Scepter slips from her fingers into Ulric's waiting hand.

"Ha ha ha!" he laughs triumphantly as he roughly pushes Livia aside. She slips halfway down the stairs, coming to rest with her head at a grotesque angle.

"Livia!" I feel ice-cold hands grip me as the Resurrected surround me. "No!"

A tremendous roar shakes the cavern as the dragon looms above the stalagmite.

"What?" Ulric gasps as the beast rears its horn-crowned head above him. "Impossible!" He waves the Scepter at the beast. "Be gone!" he orders.

The dragon roars again, acrid-smelling blood oozing from the wounds in its neck.

"Draconis!" He waves his left hand at the beast and flames erupt from the underside of the dragon's scaly neck.

It shrieks. Smoke is issuing from its mouth even as it lunges at the sorcerer.

"No!" Ulric screams as the dragon devours him in a single bite.

Rearing up on its hinds legs, the dragon roars again. Its eyes blaze with the unholy fires of the Christian Hell, and then it slowly topples from the stalagmite to crash onto the muddy ground with a final resounding crash that shakes the entire cavern.

"The Scepter!" Livia gasps as she struggled to her feet. "Where is it?"

The entire cavern is still shaking.

Weapons slip from lifeless fingers. The Resurrected collapse to the ground like discarded rags.

I wave at Livia. "We must flee!" I shout as the ground continues to shake. "The ceiling could collapse at any moment." More rocks are falling, splashing down into the mud.

"The Scepter!" she repeats, looking around desperately. "Where is it, Franc? I must have it!"

Truth be told, I want it too.

"We can restore thy lover!" Livia reminds me in her best pleading tone. "Together, the things that we can do with it are beyond count!"

"To hold him in my arms again...." The thought is so tempting. I look at the dragon's corpse. I could slice the beast's gullet and draw the Scepter from within. Shadow's Kiss would make short work of those scales I know. The thought of waving the bloody thing above my head and calling the spirit of my love back from beyond the Veil is tangible.

A large boulder crashes down mere paces from where I stand. Mud splatters my torn tunic.

"Livia, we must flee!" I shout. The near-miss is an awakening for me.

She stands, staring at the dragon. Its body is smoldering now, smoke seeping from between every scale. Foul, acrid smoke which stings my eyes and burns my throat.

"Livia!" I set foot upon the stalagmite and than lose my balance as the stone cracks asunder.

Livia cries out and falls to the ground.

I grab her wrist and haul her roughly to her feet.

"I will not be manhandled in such a fashion!" she tells me in her most haughty of tones. It amuses me to hear such anger in her voice...even as the world crashes down around us, she still clings to her ladylike persona.

"We can discuss this later," I tell her as I pulled her towards the tunnel. "We must flee else we shall be crushed."

"But, the Scepter," she protests helplessly.

"'Tis lost to us now." The mud sucks at our boots. "We must flee, Livia." I tug at her arm.

Fortune, and the gods, favour us and somehow we escape from the tunnels ere they collapse.

Actually, we had luck for the shaking had collapsed many of the walls allowing us a more direct route in which to flee back to the surface world. Even as we stumble into the clearing from which we first had entered the mountain, Ymir's Fang erupts in fire and flame.

Livia stares at the rocks which now block the tunnel through which we had journeyed into the frost giant's heart.

"'Tis over."

"Aye." Livia kicks at one small rock with her booted foot. "Lost to us, Franc!" she snarls. "We had the most powerful talisman in our hands and now 'tis lost to us!"

"The talisman be not everything," I remind her as another tremor shakes the ground under our feet. "There be other important things in the world. Things not borne of magick. Friendship for one."

She stares at me in silence for what feels like hours. "We could have been gods," she moans, turning back to beseechingly gaze at the mountain.

"We are already more than mortal," I remind her. "And we already lay claim to a greater share of immortality than most can dream of." I take her arm and slowly lead her towards our tethered horses. "Might I accompany thee back to thy lands in the south, my Lady?" I ask. The neighing of the scared horses trying to break free of their hobbles mars the effect I have been hoping to achieve.

She eyes the terrified horses for a moment as they rear and pull at the ropes binding them.

"Aye, my Lord." Regaining her courtly airs, she accepts my arm. "Lead on."

###

About the author:

Born and raised in small-town Ontario, Matt Kirkby is a romantic dreamer who specializes in writing tales of high fantasy and pulp-style science fiction and space operas. He draws his inspiration from all diverse sources and ideas: Science Fiction, Fantasy, Gothic Horror, Pastoral Nature.

He started his writing career submitting fan fiction for numerous *Star Wars* and *TransFormers* fanzines, but has since moved on to writing professionally.

He published his first novel, <u>A Wyrm In The Heart</u> in 2004.

He lives a double life, writing classy sci-fi and fantasy for fun under his own name, and penning gay erotica under the pen name of Frank Sol.

When not writing, Matt spends his time helping his partner with his hand-crafted rocking chair business -- <u>Off Your Rocker</u> -- and trying to maintain some control over his cat. He still thinks that no gift is better than a new book.

Connect with Me Online:

Smashwords: http://www.smashwords.com/profile/ view/MattKirkby

Follow on Twitter— https://twitter.com/talonspiritcat

Facebook: http://facebook.com/ MattKirkby

Also by Matt Kirkby

A Novel of Lovecraftian Horror
The Death of Hope

Standalone
A Wyrm In the Heart

About the Author

Born and raised in small-town Ontario, Matt Kirkby is a romantic dreamer who specializes in writing tales of high fantasy and pulp-style science fiction and space operas. He draws his inspiration from all diverse sources and ideas: Science Fiction, Fantasy, Gothic Horror, Pastoral Nature. He started his writing career submitting fan fiction for numerous Star Wars and TransFormers fanzines, but has since moved on to writing professionally. He published his first novel, A Wyrm In The Heart in 2004. He lives a double life, writing classy sci-fi and fantasy for fun under his own name, and penning gay erotica under the pen name of Frank Sol. When not writing, Matt spends his time helping his partner with his hand-crafted rocking chair business -- www.OffYourRocker.ca -- and trying to maintain some control over his cat. He still thinks that no gift is better than a new book.